D0261425

Snow
and Other Stories

Snow and Other Stories

BY ANTONY LAMBTON

Quartet Books
London Melbourne New York

Dedicated to
LUCY, BEATRIX, ROSE, ANNE, ISABELLA
and NED

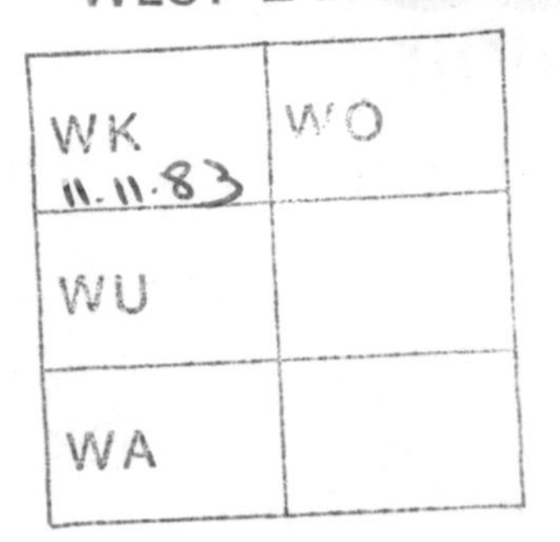

First published by Quartet Books Limited 1983
A member of the Namara Group
27/29 Goodge Street, London WIP 1FD

British Library Cataloguing in Publication Data

Lambton, Antony
Snow and other stories.
I. Title.
823'.914[F] PR6062.A/

ISBN 0-7043-2407-5

Typeset by A.K.M. Associates (U.K.) Ltd., Southall, London
Printed and bound in Great Britain
by Mackays of Chatham Ltd., Kent

Contents

SNOW
AND OTHER STORIES

BY ANTONY LAMBTON

Quartet Books
London Melbourne New York

Dedicated to
LUCY, BEATRIX, ROSE, ANNE, ISABELLA
and NED

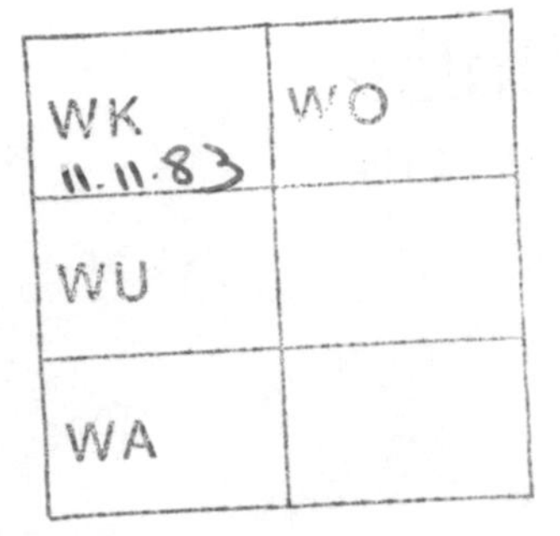

First published by Quartet Books Limited 1983
A member of the Namara Group
27/29 Goodge Street, London WIP 1FD

British Library Cataloguing in Publication Data

Lambton, Antony
Snow and other stories.
I. Title.
823'.914[F] PR6062.A/

ISBN 0-7043-2407-5

Typeset by A.K.M. Associates (U.K.) Ltd., Southall, London
Printed and bound in Great Britain
by Mackays of Chatham Ltd., Kent

Contents

Foreword

This stimulating medley of short stories brings to mind an eclectic art collection in which oil paintings, pastels, water colours and etchings are discriminatingly displayed on the walls of a spacious gallery, and they are refreshing for their variety of scene and subject. Their settings range from Richmond to Tsarist Russia.

Whether in an oil painting ('1 August 1918') or in a delicate water colour ('Charlotte Gwynne') the author remains a versatile virtuoso, never laying on his pigments too heavily as in the case of most modern short stories, which are sprinkled with obscenities for the sake of a bogus realism. Lord Lambton can convince us of reality without such aids, and create changes of atmosphere without laborious descriptions. Indeed, he is a chameleon of atmosphere, yet his style is simple and straightforward: there is no sense of strain.

'1 August 1918', the strongest and most ironical story in the book, is typical of what happened to many a progressive landowner during the Russian Revolution. Even on an estate 'remote from the backwaters of provincial life' the pitiless steamroller destroyed the remnants of a noble family who had always cared for their dependants. The paternalistic liberal Prince Dimitri Ivanovitch Kropotkin is a Tolstoyan figure, and his weak son Prince Pavel is a traditional type of Slav fatalist whom Chekhov has made familiar. The peasants who prostrate themselves before executing Prince Pavel and his wife, who might have escaped but for the fact that the Princess's spaniel was having puppies ('They could not take her with them on a journey in such a condition or the puppies might die'), are true to the serf mentality. After liquidating the harmless couple the shooting party shuffle off to the tavern Prince Pavel had built for the peasants, 'to celebrate the end of the bad old days and the birth of a new system based on brotherly love, equality, justice and fair shares for all men'. The bare narrative is as effective as a tale by Mérimée.

A complete contrast with this lurid chapter of modern history is provided by the sharp etching of 'The Intercession' which takes us to civilized Umbria. Julia and her husband Charles, a smug martinet, on a three weeks' tour of Italy, are 'covering Assisi before lunch'. Charles, chairman of his family company, considers sightseeing a moral obligation and, like too many tourists today, keeps a dutiful eye on his watch and guide book rather than on the splendid scenery and works of art, while Julia regrets leaving her two boys at home. After a fortnight 'she had seen enough pictures' and was tired of 'packing and unpacking and the tedium of waking up with a lost useless feeling, in a series of hotel rooms'. Troubled by a premonition of death in the family and fearing for her children, she finds herself praying to Pallas Athene, alias Minerva, in a church which had originally been a pagan temple. As a result she is liberated from her priggish husband and transformed from a passive into an active matriarch.

'La Gioconda' evokes the rejuvenating influence of rural Italy on the voluptuous mother of two teenage daughters. She cannot resist an impulse to run out of doors naked to meet the dewy dawn and, possibly, a roving centaur or the great god Pan himself. But all she encounters is an aged gardener, who is almost as embarrassed as her daughters. Her illusory trysts with a pagan deity are a consolation for the advance of middle age.

Lord Lambton's ironical view of things is most evident in 'The Lunette', which deals with the conflict between aesthetic idealism and the necessity of financial profit. This was apparently suggested by the career of an eminent apostle of early Tuscan art, about whose expertise fantastic legends have gathered since the 1890s.

General knowledge of the arts has spread considerably since those palmy days for collectors when ignorant parish priests were eager to barter a brand-new copy for a dusty antique predella. As Henry James wrote: 'Every good story is of course both a picture and an idea, and the more they are interfused the better the problem is solved.' It strikes me as an accident that Lord Lambton should not have been a painter, for the pictorial character of his stories is salient. Snow has been depicted by most of the French Impressionists; for centuries it has been popular with Chinese and Japanese painters and poets as an emblem of purity, and in Europe and America it is associated with Christmas festivity. But since reading the title story of this book I doubt if I shall ever contemplate snowflakes with the same cheerful emotion. Assuredly I had not envisaged it as a dangerous secret weapon. Henceforth when I hear that it will snow I shall watch the falling flakes with apprehension, and with a lingering suspicion that the Russians may employ it against us after all. Apart from which the cloud from northern Siberia (notorious in limericks for its monastic discipline) seems symbolic of a threat to Western civilization.

Beginning with the ingredients of light comedy, the story ends in near tragedy. The large flat with a roof garden overlooking Richmond Park becomes claustrophobic when the snowfall, so welcome at first with Christmas in sight, becomes 'the heaviest in living memory', with telephones out of order, helicopters flying emergency cases, and emergency sessions in Parliament. The growing tension of the situation is admirably conveyed by the diary form in which 'Snow' is related. The BBC continues to function throughout, and the parody of official speeches is brilliantly plausible. The President of the United States comes to the defence of 'allies to whom they were ethically committed' and the 'icy feed cloud lane from Siberia' is successfully nullified just before Christmas. The tedious fellow tenants of the flat are full of humorous touches. Here one rubs one's eyes before the revelation of a fresh literary talent. A second helping, please, I hunger for more!

Harold Acton

Snow

Friday, 11 December. This is the first sentence of my second attempt at keeping a diary. My first was when, as a child, a little red tricycle appeared at the end of my bed one Christmas morning, causing me to believe that my horizons were so enlarged as to be of general interest. I asked my mother for a notebook and was given a small blue one, very similar to the one I am writing in now. I still have it. On the first day I wrote that I had ridden to the end of the garden and pedalled ten times without stopping, round the small circular drive in front of the house. I ended by saying how much time a bicycle saved. On the second day my experiences were identical. On the third day, perhaps thinking it was not interesting to repeat myself three times running, after carefully writing the date, I left the remainder of the page blank. This was the end of my first diary. Now I am determined to write every day for a year. It is a firm resolution.

The correct method of diary-writing, I read somewhere, is to conceive yourself as writing a letter to a trusted friend. The weakness of this is that a trusted friend knows you and those you are writing about. So before following this plan I shall describe my family to those who do not know us, for I hope and believe that some day somebody will read these words. I do not believe anyone has ever written a diary for themselves.

I am thirty-two and like to think I am not conscious of my looks. Until the age of seventeen or eighteen, when boys began to say I was pretty, I never knew what I looked like. Then I remember examining myself carefully from every angle in the mirror and deciding they were right. I had pitch-black hair and an olive skin with a faint undertone of natural red, dark brown eyes, very white teeth, and when I smiled in the mirror it looked like a very nice smile. I have never been shy and have always found it easy to get on with people. If you talk and say what you think people think you are clever, because most of them do not think anything at all.

My upbringing was strange. What my father's history was I do not know. He was, as my mother conveyed to me as early as I can remember, socially beneath her, and she was never forgiven by her family or herself for marrying him. He was dark, with I should think gypsy blood, mysterious, coming and going in my life with decreasing frequency and eventually retiring to a little farm in the Welsh hills where he kept sheep and repaired farm machinery. I cannot say I blame him – he must have wanted to be a long way from my mother. She was terrible, there is no other word for her. With fair hair fluffed up in front, a powder-pink face and a plump body, the prototype of suburban pretension of the 1940s. Somehow her father had made some money. She was too genteel to say how but I was given a good education, and spent as much of my holidays as possible with my friends. What I hated most about her were her unforgettable visits to my last school where she was very anxious to impress my upper-class friends and their visiting parents. So she used to arrive in a hired Rolls Royce, always addressing the driver as 'chauffeur' in tones constantly copied and repeated in my hearing. Nothing could prevent her visits and each time she would force me to take friends out to tea whom I could see memorizing her remarks for repetition. She would say goodbye, triumphant in her gentility and the good her visits had done me. I nearly died of shame every time. When I left school she had some terrible idea that I should go and finish in Paris, which did not fit in with my plans at all. I left home and for the next two years supported myself as a secretary, nursemaid, receptionist and assistant to a greyhound trainer. I enjoyed myself and resisted seduction until, when I was eighteen, I saw somebody I liked. I then had three other love affairs, none of which was serious, but all pleasant. Then I met my future husband, William, who was in the Army. I had never met anyone like him. He was funny and imaginative and the discipline perfectly complemented the brilliant disorder of his mind. Anyhow, we married and in the next two years I had two children, Lucy and Anne, who are now twelve and eleven.

Now I must describe William. He is just under six foot and at the same time rather solid-looking, like you would imagine King Edward VII looked as a young man, although old photographs show he did not. He is still as brilliant as ever but his business life has been a series of disasters. Let me tell one story which reveals his character.

After my pregnancies ended and we started going out again he bought a small factory on the way to London Airport and threw himself into the manufacture of a new dish-washing machine, the need of which he used to exhibit when we were dining with friends. With great excitement he would pick up a glass and point at the rim showing everybody the traces of lipstick; or alternatively lift up a fork and show an atom of food left between the prongs. This would delight him and he would explain to furious or embarrassed girls that it would never happen when his machine was ready. I don't know how many friends we lost by this behaviour for it is extraordinary how quickly bohemians become house-proud, and I am afraid I made things worse because I could never resist laughing at the exchange of glances between husband and wife and the quick replacement of the offending article while William beamed, full of good intentions.

Anyhow, after about two years the machine was ready and he gave a demonstration to which what he called 'the trade' was invited. The only drink provided was champagne, which was bad and hot, and I could see not at all popular. William then gave them a long lecture on the filthiness of the cutlery with which they doubtless ate, which I could see infuriated them. There was a positive rustle of indignation when he produced six plates, each one dirtier than the other, encrusted with Chum. On each was also a large bone. These combinations he put into six washing machines which, when turned on, made a whirring noise like an aeroplane revving up, so that I had to put my hands over my ears. In a remarkably short time it stopped and all the plates were perfectly clean and the bones greaseless and spotless. For a moment I could see the interest of his 'guests' was aroused, despite their having been further insulted at his apparent belief that their families ate Chum and bones. The result was certainly startling, then one of them asked the cost; the reply was at least three times the price of the most expensive machine on the market. The room emptied quickly. Three machines were sold and William lost everything he had.

At the same time my mother died and left me quite a lot of money, otherwise we would have been living on the street. On the other hand, when one of William's bizarre schemes fails, his belief in himself soon finds other backers for a similar one. He always throws himself wholeheartedly into his projects with the devotion of an idealist, never ceasing until they are perfect and unsaleable. At present, he is manufacturing a telephone which you can keep in your pocket.

As these various interests keep him engaged from morning to night I saw and see little of him and have lived the life of an unmarried girl with all the natural consequences.

However, none of these mattered until ten months ago I met Edmund with whom I fell in love, for the first time in my life. We were both married, but I have always been a romantic and did not mind not seeing him all the time as long as I knew he loved me. He is tall and dark and very determined, and honest and clever, and works for the BBC. However, that is enough about him for the moment. In any case I don't really know what he looks like or what he is like. I do not think anybody in love has the faintest idea what the loved one is like – he or she becomes a myth. I only know that I am enchanted by him.

Now to the children. Lucy is just twelve, thin, pale and very collected. She looks rather like me except that she has a whiter skin and sometimes I find her rather cold but she is pretty and charming. Anne, on the other hand, a little over a year younger, is far less formally pretty, much softer-hearted, with a round face and large mouth which breaks into the most charming smile when she is pleased, but which turns down in despair if things go wrong.

We live in a large flat in a block overlooking Richmond Park. It is one of four flats with a large roof garden. And now, tomorrow, Saturday, 12 December, I am going to start my day by day account of my life.

Saturday, 12 December. José, my Filipino maid, came at nine o'clock and took the children shopping to buy certain presents about which they are exceedingly secretive. For once sensible, William will not let them go shopping in central London alone. Anyhow, I suddenly remembered I had not finished my own Christmas shopping and spent all the morning at Harrods, Hamleys, the General Trading Company, Marks and Spencers and two expensive picture galleries. This year, because I am so happy, I have thought carefully about the children's presents and even William's, while in the galleries I have been searching for something lovely for Edmund, the source of my happiness. (I really sound sickly and sentimental.) On the other hand I dread buying crackers and a horrid little fir tree and tinsel and all the Christmas food and have kept putting it off. But hearing the children talk I saw it was very important to them – as I think it was to me – to have everything unchanged, mince pies, mistletoe, turkey and a Christmas pudding with flaming brandy. All must be as before.

I came back laden with parcels in a hired car. Otherwise there was no way I could carry everything, and I could not have parked had I driven myself. The children were very pleased with themselves about their secret presents and were sweet at lunch.

Afterwards José went home and, as it was a lovely day, I decided to take the children and Daisy, who is our Alsatian dog, for a walk in Richmond Park. The children pretended I was their chauffeur and sat in the back with the dog. It was a very noisy journey as they kept pointing out dogs in the street which made Daisy bark almost continuously. It was a relief to get out at the Twin Ponds car park. Despite my telling her not to, Lucy at once started throwing a ball for Daisy which made her go flying about and terrifying several people who thought she was attacking them rather than the ball. As we were walking between the two ponds Lucy and Anne saw two of their school friends carrying an enormous kite. At once there came over their faces the guilty look I have often seen before when they think they ought to stay with me but long to do something else. I thought it was nice of them to feel like that and told them to run along, I would meet them in exactly an hour and a quarter by Anne's watch. I felt a glow of satisfaction at my unselfishness until I decided this was pure hypocrisy as I wished to be alone.

Setting off up the hill I felt so happy I imitated the children and threw a stick for Daisy. She wouldn't play with me and walked about in a responsible manner, sometimes giving a rather unpleasant look at the deer. One of the great advantages of owning an Alsatian is the fear it inspires. At one point I thought I was going to be troubled by one of those odd men who walk about alone, wearing a mackintosh and stand under oak trees in the park. One of them took a step or two towards me, saw Daisy, stopped dead and went back under his tree. I always feel sorry for these men; I cannot imagine they have much success and the mackintoshes must be very hot in summer and cold in winter. Also it must be boring hanging about endlessly under trees.

Leaving him behind I walked up the hill and around the fence, in the shade. The bracken was still crisp and white with frost and the oak leaves felt pleasant to walk on. I began to feel reflective and started to think about Edmund. It is said a lover comes between a woman and children and ruins her marriage. All I can say is that my lover has made mine. I was not happy before I met him, and casual relationships had ceased to interest me. I know I am nicer to the children now because I am happy. Before they were a part of my general frustration. I think I am also more tolerant of William. We had never been close since we first married and I had come to regard him as a lunatic, never bothering to please him because it did not seem worth the effort. Now, on the other hand, I think of him as a human being, an unhappy misplaced genius, and I go out of my way to be considerate. I think he is pleased, although he would never admit as much. Suddenly it occurred to me that perhaps I was nicer to my husband and children because I felt guilty. But I decided that no, I don't feel guilty but happy, and one is certainly not truly happy if one feels guilt. I spent the remaining hour of my freedom luxuriously thinking of Edmund, of what we had done, what we were going to do, where I would be able to find a water colour I know he would love for Christmas.

The children had been enthralled by their kite-flying and talked loudly to one another, looking hard at me, about how lovely it would be if kind Father Christmas gave them one each in their stocking. I said I had heard them and would see if I could get in touch with him. The excursion had been a great success and on the way back even Daisy was quiet. It was as if even she were determined not to spoil the success of the afternoon.

The spell was broken by Simmonds, the hall porter or concierge, as he calls himself, coming out of his poky little flat with an ingratiatingly false smile and two toffee apples. I hate him. He is unpleasant and unhelpful for eleven and a half months of the year, and then just before Christmas starts sucking up to remind us of his Christmas box. For the last four years I have given him two bottles, one of whisky and one of gin. He will be drunk and maudlin for the holiday period, then revert to his unpleasant self again.

Toffee apples are the most disgusting, sticky things, breaking into bits and attaching themselves to everything. However, luckily the children seemed to have grown out of them and I had to pinch Lucy to thank him. Upstairs they threw them away without even tasting them, saying his apples were always green and bitter.

It had been cold in the park and the flat looks very welcoming since I put in one of those imitation gas fires which look real. I asked the children to get tea and walked out into the roof garden, luckily choosing exactly that moment of a frosty, sunny day when the sky lights up and glows for perhaps a minute before darkness comes. The roof is nicer now because the beech hedge I planted hides the flat iron railings and makes it look more like the real thing. The frost was making all the lights sparkle and I cannot help thinking how silly it is when people say money does not make happiness; it does. I do not want a yacht or anything silly like that but I do love my quarter of the roof garden. What adds to its charm is the mystery of what happens over the dividing wall in the next garden which belongs to a man called Stephens who is never seen although important-looking people very occasionally call. He has a faded, worried-looking wife. Once I even got as far as piling two wine boxes on top of each other to stand on and see over, but thought I would feel such an idiot if I found myself looking him in the face that I had second thoughts, or rather did not dare. Now I think ignorance is more romantic. It would be disappointing if instead of the exotic plants I imagine as spreading everywhere, there were just empty unattended grass. I once found the children trying to look over by piling a box on a chair but I stopped them and said it was a mystery and they were not to try and solve it. The mystery remains, for I have never heard a sound from the other side.

After we had finished some burnt toast which they said was delicious when you scraped the black off, I read two chapters from *Wind in the Willows.*

Anne was frightened and squashed against me gripping my arm but Lucy, logical as ever, said: 'Of course I would be frightened if I were lost in a snow storm in a wild wood but I am not. I am in a warm room, sitting in front of a fire.'

At half past seven William came back from the factory in a very good mood, loudly declaring that in two years everybody will be carrying telephones like they now carry fountain pens. I resisted the impulse to say that few carry pens now. We had avocado pears and risotto for dinner as he is now a vegetarian.

Soon afterwards we went to bed and I wrote this diary. I am glad I have started. And now I am going to turn the light off and think of my beloved and hope I dream of him as well. I feel in a lovely soppy mood but cannot help wondering whether all women write as nauseously as I do when they are in love.

Sunday, 13 December. I woke up early and climbing out of bed looked in the mirror which reassured me and made me decide to make it as nice a day as possible for everybody. I knew what Lucy would like to do because the children now have a Sunday morning ritual getting their cereals and milk and sugar and going back to have breakfast in bed while they talk about the events of the week and their plans. Sometimes I eavesdrop. I am sure they realize and talk a little louder so that I can hear how sophisticated they are. Twice Lucy has said how much she longs to go to Brighton where a friend of hers lives in a Regency house with a round front and balconies. I thought for some time as to how on earth I could make William want to go.

At last an idea came to me and, calling Lucy, I said: 'One of the cleverest things you can do in life is to have a plan yourself and make others believe it is theirs. Now I know you want to go to Brighton and so do I, so what we have to do is make Daddy feel the same way. Go into his room, look as sad as you can and say, "Please, Daddy, Mummy promised we could go to Brighton for a treat. Now she says she does not want to go. Please make her." '

She repeated what she had to say, laughed and went into her father's room. The plan worked very well. There was an indignant roar and two minutes later William came bounding in, holding up his pyjama trousers. 'What's this, what's this?' he shouted, delighted to simulate fury, 'breaking promises to children as well? Why not go to Brighton? Beautiful town, sun, sand and sea air, do them the world of good and, what's more,' he added, 'I want to consult Professor Collins who lives there. Certainly we shall go.'

'Of course I will if you want to,' I said quietly, 'but I didn't know you liked Brighton.'

'Why not, why not?' he shouted, 'and what's more, you idiot, unless we hurry we'll not catch the ten o'clock train.' He turned and rushed out of the room.

Lucy gave me a conspiratorial smile. I hope she has learned a useful lesson.

After a terrific rush we caught the ten-thirty and arrived in Brighton just after twelve. For some inexplicable reason, Will had a pair of race-glasses slung over his shoulder. I did not ask him what they were for; it was more fun trying to imagine. He left us as soon as we had walked out of the station and, telling me to book a table at the Golden Grill, said he would meet us there at half past one. Afterwards we went down on the beach and looked out to sea. There were some very odd-shaped ships on the horizon. Being winter, nearly all the entertainments were closed, but it didn't matter as it was such a lovely day.

Then we decided to explore some of the little old streets behind the front. At once we saw a dirty sign in a dirty window announcing that fortunes were told. The children became very excited so we went and knocked on the door and were ushered into a dirty little sitting room by a nervous girl with long dirty black hair. In the waiting room the chairs and sofas were so greasy that we instinctively perched on the edges and waited until the little girl peeped round another door and asked one of us to go in. Lucy went first and came out after a few minutes looking cross and said the fortune teller was still half asleep and her eyes had been closed while she was pretending to be staring in a crystal ball. Lucy had nudged her foot and the fat woman had jumped and told her that she was going to cross water very soon.

'That's right,' Lucy replied, 'I will have to cross the Thames to get home tonight, won't I?'

'Now dear,' said the woman, 'if you're going to be pert go and get your sister, and we will see if she isn't a wiser little girl.'

Anne stayed quite a long time and came out looking mysterious, refusing to say what she had been told except that it might be important. I wanted to pay and leave, but the children insisted I should go in. A fat woman was sitting in front of a crystal. She sat so long without saying anything that I began to think Lucy was right and that she was still asleep.

At length she said: 'I see a fair handsome man in your life.'

'No,' I said, 'he's not fair, he's dark,' at which she cackled and continued looking at me out of the corners of her eyes. 'Well, I see a handsome man, anyhow, and he is going to play a big part in your future.'

She seized my hand and started to rub my palms with an unpleasant movement halfway between a caress and a massage. I did not like it at all, pulled away and paid her nine pounds, thinking it had not been a waste of time and money because it had been amusing.

At lunch, which I paid for, as it was my treat, William and the children had double helpings of smoked salmon which they love and I made him tell them about Prince Regent and Beau Brummell and the Pavilion where I thought I would take them after we had called on Lucy's friend. As usual, he was very well informed and amusing and lovable as only he can be when he is not excited or in a bad temper. After the crêpes suzettes we went to pay our call.

The parents were rather nice. He, apparently, was a well-known writer and I could see he expected me to know who he was although I had never heard of him. His wife was pretty and friendly and said another time to tell her earlier and come to lunch. I asked what else was open that would amuse the children; the daughter, Natasha, said 'the waxworks'. Relieved to get away from the politeness and formalities, Lucy and Natasha behaving as if they had never met, we followed correctly various complicated directions. I paid at the door but the children would not allow me to go in for a minute or two as they wanted to cover up the labels to test my general knowledge. It was a great success. Not one of the images looked like anyone I had ever seen and the children were entranced when I guessed that a villainous-looking fat man with a bludgeon in his hand was Charles Peace. It turned out to be Winston Churchill holding a cigar. They clapped their hands and said they had no idea I was so ignorant. We caught the five o'clock back and Will was very pleased: while waiting for us in the Pavilion he met one of the three men who had bought one of his washing machines. He had said it was worth every penny he had paid for it. I asked him how Professor Collins had been. He said very well in a doubtful voice, but the mystery of the race-glasses remains unexplained.

When we got home the children hugged me and said they would never forget how lovely the sea was in the morning, and how ignorant I was not recognizing Winston Churchill in the afternoon. I have just let Daisy out on the roof where I have carefully trained her to make messes in the flower-beds. It was a lovely night and much warmer.

Monday, 14 December. My alarm clock woke me up at seven o'clock as the children had to start their last week at school. It is a dreaded week as Thursday is prize-giving day which does not interest the children much. I never won a thing at school and they have followed in their mother's footsteps, so it is a pointless day full of polite, insincere conversation. I was reassured to think it was, as far as I knew, the only nasty thing ahead.

Looking out of the window I was amazed to see that there were about six inches of snow on the ground and that it was still falling slowly in enormous flakes. As I watched a terrific gust of wind came, and in a moment the snow was blowing vertically. The children were of course delighted. They only had two hundred yards to walk, and I watched them ploughing through the snow in their gumboots.

William left at eight-thirty as he was taking the ten o'clock to Paris to see his mother, or so he said. He was angry at the snow as he hates waiting at airports. The next thing to upset him was his failure to find his galoshes, ridiculous rubber casings which he wears over his shoes and which nobody else has worn for forty years. Of course he blamed me for having mislaid them, but I thought of Edmund and asked him vaguely what could I have wanted them for, to which he had no reply except that I was a fool of a woman. Anyhow, he got off about ten o'clock wearing one galosh, grumbling that at any rate his right foot would remain dry, and I was relieved to hear on the one o'clock news that despite nine inches of snow there was so far only a two-hour delay at London Airport.

José was very late arriving, not getting here until half past eleven. It is not the sort of thing she minds, and in a sing-song voice said, 'Traffic very very delayed', so that it sounded like the first words of a song.

I felt rather sad after lunch. Monday is one of Edmund's days but he is in America and so I won't see him until Friday which seems a very long time. I made up my mind not to think of him and went through all the bills checking that I did not have to buy anything else for Christmas and that all the food, wine etc. was in the larder. This was very tedious and took a surprisingly long time.

The children came back at five o'clock and said there were at least fifteen inches of snow and that it had gone over the top of their gumboots and their feet were frozen. I turned on the weather forecast; a maddening man came on and in a self-satisfied way pointed out a lot of lines on the map and said there was a low depression centred over the whole of the British Isles – as if we did not know – extending to the north of France and the east of Ireland, which was having its heaviest snowfall in living memory. He was evasive about the future but seemed to suggest it would continue snowing and that the pattern of the cloud formation was incomprehensible. On the news it said that in the north of Scotland, where the snow is coming from, there are up to thirty-six inches and many electric lines are down. Railways north of Peterborough are now at a standstill and London Airport closed at one o'clock. William rang from Paris to say he had arrived safely. How lucky! I cannot imagine anything worse than being snowed up with him.

The children were absolutely fascinated and said that with any luck, if it went on, they would get off the rest of the term and I would get off speech day as half the children had not turned up that morning.

They kept going to the garden window, pressing their faces against the glass and shouting, 'It's still snowing, it's still snowing!'

I certainly have never known anything like it. It would not have been so bad if there had not been two hours – one in the morning, one in the evening – of gale force winds. Already there is chaos in the hospitals and helicopters are flying emergency cases all over the place. Anyhow, I am tired now.

Tuesday, 15 December. I woke up at seven with the feeling that something was wrong. It was still dark and on opening the window I could see huge flakes of snow still coming down. I got breakfast ready for the girls but there seemed so much snow outside it did not seem possible that the roads could be open, so I thought I would not wake them until I had rung up the school. The telephone was dead. The next problem was how to get Daisy out on to the roof because, when I opened the window, there were about two and a half feet of snow. I pushed my way through and made a trench through which she disappeared. My next fear was should she fall over the edge. She came back in a minute.

I heard the eight o'clock news and there seemed to be chaos everywhere; practically every side road in England closed as well as great stretches of the A1 and M1 and M4. It really is annoying that the only time William might be useful he isn't here. The snow ploughs have somehow managed to get round and the men in the other flats have formed a team and dug a trench to the street, which is still open to traffic.

When I had found all this out I woke the children up and gave them breakfast and said I would go to school with them to find out if it was shut and take them home if it was. I could not think of anything else to do and felt like doing something. The school-mistress was worried out of her life. All telephones in the area are out of order and she had no idea if any of the children who set out this morning have not arrived, and no way of finding out.

The BBC announced while we were there that all programmes had been changed and that advice to specific areas would be broadcast every half-hour. It suggested everybody should listen. The local Sainsbury's was only about a hundred yards from the school, so we went on there. Only three or four people seemed to be serving and, strangely enough, very few buying, so I loaded a trolley with every conceivable thing, and we staggered home with as much as we could carry. It was hard work. We were back at eleven. There is nothing worse than children when they have nothing to do, so I made them get out their school books and translate passages from French to English and from English to French – I would not know if their mathematical answers were right – which took us up to luncheon.

I hate a broken telephone, especially now.

In the afternoon I let the children watch a flickering television. The most appalling scenes. Helicopters working all round the clock, and apparently in the Welsh hills, Scotland and the Pennine Chain thousands and thousands of animals have been buried. There is to be an emergency session in Parliament tomorrow, though apparently a lot of MPs are snowed up in the country. The Home Secretary has made an appeal to those who do not have children to make themselves available at certain centres to help the old. Gas and electricity seem to be coming through, but outside London and the big cities – where all the lines are underground – overhead lines are down and everybody is without light, and dependent for heating on their own stores of coal and oil.

This extraordinary wind has struck again twice today – from about twelve to one this morning, fortunately after we were back, and again from six to seven this evening. The drifts are simply enormous, fifteen feet high in places. We had tinned soup for dinner as nobody was hungry. I sent the children to bed in a bad mood. The trouble is that there are no other children in the block except two boys of about fifteen on the first floor who are too old for them.

The big late night news was that Sir Frederick Barnett interrupted the Prime Minister as she was winding up in the foreign affairs debate to ask if the weather is due to Russian intervention. He also asked if Intelligence had reported that the Russians have been experimenting with weather control for a long period, and did this demonstration of power relate to the deployment of Cruise Two missiles?

He was ruled to be out of order, but afterwards the Prime Minister was quoted as saying, 'I cannot comment yet.'

How ghastly if we are all to be snowed to death. So I turned the wireless on – the television is so bad – no weather forecast tonight as contact had been broken with Bracknell, but the various experts were giving their views. I cannot understand scientific jargon but the meaning appears comprehensible. American Intelligence has received confirmed reports of successful Russian weather experimentation (a new word!) in Siberia. All the commentators pointed out that the Prime Minister had said 'no comment' when asked for an opinion of Sir Frederick's question, and Downing Street will not comment. What is extraordinary is how quickly it has all happened. Only yesterday the children were going to school and thinking it a joke, and now we are caught out in a war. The country is literally paralysed.

A late night programme on how the Russians are able to produce snow here. As nobody knew the answer a waste of time!

Wednesday, 16 December. I woke up to hear the six o'clock news for the first time in my life. It has not stopped snowing for one minute. It is now estimated that in the south of England there has been a level fall of five feet, and in the north far more. The number of people lost in cars is unknown. Telephone communications are non-existent. Nobody seems to know what is happening and the local regional wireless stations are being used as communication centres. All television stations have closed down. Many people are thought to have died – even in hospitals – of cold and food shortages have become a danger. The Prime Minister is to make a statement in London at eleven o'clock. America announced that the President will be making a statement at three p.m. Greenwich time, nine a.m. American time.

I had a curious reaction to the news of a possible food shortage. Going quickly into the larder and getting all the tins of food I could find I hid them in the bookcase. It was as if I had a sixth sense that something was going to happen. The children were nearly driving me mad, and the only person who is no trouble is Daisy who just jumps out into a hole in the snow and comes back again.

We are now totally snowed in and the only exit – a tunnel under the snow – leads to the street, which is now blocked. I let the children sleep as long as possible and then gave them more French to do. Lucy started complaining and I smacked her on the head. She looked amazed. I was furious with myself, said sorry and kissed her, but she looked terribly hurt.

At eleven o'clock the Prime Minister spoke, explaining that she had to say 'no comment' last night because all the reports were not yet in and she had not yet had full consultations with the President. Since then weather experts all over the world, without a single exception, have given their opinion that the cloud formation, starting in Siberia and extending over the British Isles, northern France and the east of Ireland, cannot have been formed by nature, nor can it conceivably have been created by our allies. She said she had informed the President that in her opinion this weather assault was an act of war. Already countless numbers of men, women and children had died. The Soviet Union was, by insidious methods, attempting to prevent the deployment next month of Cruise Two missiles in the United Kingdom:

'We have been informed by neutral sources that in the event of Her Majesty's Government informing the United States that these missiles would not be deployed, the snowfall would stop. According to our information, reliable neutral sources have informed the President of the United States that if he announces a cancellation of the Cruise Two missiles, due to be stationed in Europe in the spring, the weather will change.' The Prime Minister continued, 'Her Majesty's Government cannot agree to accede to blackmail, despite the hardship, sorrow and agony that the weather is causing England.'

However, she realizes that while the Government holds this opinion the opposition disagrees and it would be wrong not to debate the matter. She has therefore approached the French Government with a request that they provide seating facilities for a meeting of Parliament. They have agreed and made available the Vendôme Palace. So far three hundred and three Members of Parliament in and around London have been contacted, one hundred of whom are snowed up in Westminster (the rest are missing). They are to be flown out by helicopter for an undisclosed destination. The heads of the Services are remaining in the United Kingdom and the Cabinet will also remain in London, but will travel by helicopters for the debate planned tomorrow.

She ended by saying that obviously the easy way out was to give in, but she 'would ask the country to remember that paying the *Danegeld* is seldom productive of anything except further demands. This homeland has suffered hardship before and survived. It is now suffering in a different way and I believe I speak for the country as a whole in stating that while to give in now might seem momentarily advantageous it would, in the long term, be disastrous. We have to see it through.'

The children heard and sat looking stunned. Anne suddenly said, 'Mummy, are we going to be killed?'

I know I paused a minute before I said no, and both of them suddenly became very quiet and went away together.

A moment later there was a knock on the front door. I could not conceive who would be calling at this hour, but on opening it found myself faced by two occupants of lower flats whom I barely know by sight. One was a little, black-haired, sharp-eyed civil servant of some kind who is married to the rich, pretty daughter of a German industrialist, the other was also a civil servant called Sir Thomas Flack, retired now, who was Permanent Secretary in some Ministry or other, whatever that means.

They had behind them the hall porter – I could not help noticing that he looked self-satisfied – and two boys of fifteen and sixteen about whom I know nothing except that they are called Thompson and live on the third floor. The dominant member of this little group, the black-haired civil servant, introduced himself to me as Robert Chase and said doubtless I had heard the appeal by the Home Secretary last night for economies of every kind. A block committee had therefore been established consisting of four men and four women. He corrected himself, ladies. I could have hit him. Their first decision, which they hoped I would agree was right, was that there should be a general pooling of all food resources, and as Flat Three was by chance empty, it had been designated a communal eating place to provide morning and evening meals. I asked why a meeting had not been called before the decision to commandeer our food was made. Chase said smoothly that last night he had gone round and asked eleven flat occupants for their agreement. All had given it. However, this had taken until one o'clock and he had not wished to disturb me so late, but he was sure I would not object to what was obviously for the common good.

I said I supposed not and took them into the kitchen and gave them everything except the turkey and plum pudding and the Christmas day food, and some tea and cheese which I insisted on keeping and, of course, the unknown tins of soup, spaghetti etc. behind the books. Chase marked everything with little sticky bits of paper with my name on. I could not understand why this ridiculous messing was necessary and walked up and down in anger. It is obvious that there will be some contact between America and Russia within the next few days, and either Russia will stop the snowfall or America will agree not to place their Cruise Two missiles here. Of course, during this period more people are going to die but the Government must believe, and I think they are right, that if we give in now various sorts of blackmail will continue until Europe becomes a Russian satellite. On the other hand there is the increasingly powerful peace lobby in the United States and the last thing they want is a nuclear war initiated by themselves, so it looks as if we may have to give in. Anyhow, we are snowed in and as it is Christmas, everyone has enough food to last for a week or two, so why play at Communists ourselves? I believe it is that love of self-sacrifice which English people have. In any case, having communal meals and talking to these dreary people who are all rich and silly will be unendurable. I will certainly speak at the meeting this evening.

I gave the children some tinned spaghetti and soup for lunch. They did not eat very much, so I told them not to worry as they would not be killed. We would either give in or they would give in. An enormous look of relief came over their faces. Fortunately, they are still at the age when they think their parents are full of wisdom.

At three o'clock the President spoke to Europe. He stated that the depression which had formed over the United Kingdom was created by what he called 'an icy feed cloud lane from Siberia' –

satellite pictures were shown of a huge cloud like a fat snake leading from Siberia with us at the head – by methods not totally, he repeated the word 'totally', comprehended by American scientists.

He was convinced that the abnormal fall of snow was an anti-social weapon which he did not and could not say was not a weapon of war. The United States could not stand by and see their allies – to whom they were committed by past and present bonds of democracy and freedom – destroyed by a perversion of nature into a weapon as deadly as any ever conceived by man. Otherwise it would be Britain first, France second, Germany third, and maybe the USA fourth, so he would like Europe to know that the representative of the United States in Moscow has conveyed to the President of the USSR in no uncertain terms, that while there still remains further time for talking, 'time is now limited'. The American Government had always stated they would not deploy Cruise Two missiles in Europe unless these were opposed by numbers of similar missiles as at present.

The President ended by saying very slowly, 'The situation has never been so dangerous and, in certain circumstances, if the USSR continues to snow to death the British nation, the United States and her allies would have to take certain military steps to prevent the completion of the destruction which has already begun. Speaking for myself, the last thing I want is war. Speaking for the people of the United States the last thing they want is war. Speaking for the peoples of the world, including those nations which cannot freely speak for themselves, the last thing they want is war. It therefore rests with the President of the USSR to end this new method of warfare which is as deadly as it is unethical and which, if continued, could endanger the peace of the world.'

I wonder what he meant. Anyhow, we shall see.

After his broadcast we had a so-called meeting at five o'clock. I had never realized how dreadful my co-tenants were. Apart from Chase's wife who is blonde and very pretty and a couple who are the parents of those two boys, called Thompson, who appeared human, the rest were old men who looked as if they lived in tissue paper, and women who looked as if they lived in beauty parlours without being made beautiful, with the exception of a strident woman wearing jodhpurs who looks after the garden for pleasure.

There was no platform, for there was no wood, but three chairs were placed at the end of the room, with Sir Thomas Flack sitting in the centre as Chairman, flanked on his right by Chase and on his left by the jodhpured gardener representing the female sex.

Flack got up and in an unctuous voice welcomed everyone saying that with perhaps one exception – and here he glanced at me – we had all accepted the necessity of food-sharing in the national interest. Flat Three, as we could see, was spacious and the room in which we were sitting would be used for all meals, a rota of ladies were prepared to cook, a rota of men to wash up. This plan had been accepted by all flat-occupants with one exception – another nasty look at me – and today (or rather, this afternoon, he added with a wink as if he was telling a joke) he wished to discuss what we could do for the good of the community as a whole. We were perfectly willing to take in the homeless but there did not appear to be any in the neighbourhood, and as the roads were now altogether blocked, so was our capacity to help.

The next question was power. As far as he understood, the electric power stations in London had several weeks' supply of fuel, and as the communication lines were underground there was no immediate danger of a shortage, especially as the Government had stationed troops in emergency quarters to ensure movement of fuel. Nevertheless, as it was always wise to save as much as possible, a box had been placed at the end of the room to which everybody had consigned their Christmas candles. The number was surprisingly large.

'You never know what you have until you look for it,' said Sir Thomas in his witty way, and one or two of the women laughed.

'And it is suggested that electric light should be only used in one room at a time and candles used in all bedrooms. We feel that by doing this we are at least making our little contribution.'

I could hardly sit still at this nonsense. Then Chase got up and said lists of eating hours had been made out, and that menus would be printed and stuck up and so on. He hoped everyone would agree and work together for the common good. Then the jodhpured lady spoke and said it reminded her of the war when she had been a land girl which had given her a taste for gardening. She felt if we all pulled together we would come through like last time, but it was for us all to do our little bit, as a lot of little bits made a big bit. She sat down and all the women clapped enthusiastically and the men politely.

I could not stand it any more and burst out, 'I really object to being looked at as if I was refusing to help. Nobody has asked me to cook. I am perfectly willing to if asked. But I cannot help thinking we are all wasting time. The President said only two hours ago we are on the brink of a momentous war. Either he is serious or he is bluffing. If he is serious they will give in, if he is bluffing he will probably give in, so what is the point of us creating a little Communist state to combat a brutal Communist act, which will not help anybody in any way? Why push us all together, take us out of our rooms and try to give us some sort of team spirit? It is ridiculous. I am ready to help in any way, but would much rather have my meals with my children and hear the wireless in my own room than be dragooned down here and get on your nerves and you on mine.' I sat down.

There was a sort of uneasy shuffling silence as though I had been a spoil-sport, and then Flack got up and said he 'never liked to contradict a lady, especially a beautiful lady', but he personally was not irritated by getting to know his fellow tenants, indeed it seemed to him he had missed a great deal by not meeting them earlier, as he found it interesting to make new friends, and more fun than sitting alone boring his wife with his old stories.

The great thing was surely for us not to fall out, and here he put a wealth of sincerity in his voice. 'If the charming lady does not like our arrangements I have a tray and she can have her food put on it and her children can carry it up to her, and we will all be happy. There is one thing you learn being a civil servant which is that most matters can be settled civilly.'

This was greeted by a storm of applause. I just smiled at everyone and said when could I cook, which seemed to annoy them. I was told all meals were booked for the next ten days so my help was not needed. I said to tell me if there was anything for me to do, but nobody said anything.

A funny thing happened this afternoon about an hour after the meeting. There was another knock on the door and I wondered if it was that beastly little Chase again. But it was the two Thompson boys, who had come to see the girls. I was astonished when I saw them and then I thought, or rather knew, that they just wanted something to do so I said yes, come in, do you play cards? As they said no, I told the girls to teach them 'Hearts'. They seemed to talk for hours together and did not leave until about seven when they asked if they could come back tomorrow. I saw Lucy and Anne looking anxious so I said, 'Of course, whenever you like.'

It is very strange as boys of fifteen and sixteen usually hate girls of eleven and twelve. I suppose they want to know what girls – even young girls – are like before they are killed.

Well, the girls went down and fetched supper at seven o'clock, an hour at which I hate eating. The food was cold and very nasty so I tried to remember who was cooking but the children seemed revived and ate everything while I had a bit of cheese. The news in the evening was alarming. The leader of the opposition, now in Paris, and the deputy leader of the Liberal Party – the leader was last heard of under a thirty-foot drift in Selkirk – both demanded that Britain should refuse to accept Cruise Two missiles. Further furious peace protests in the United States, a demonstration outside the White House and others in several cities. Parliament is now meeting in the Vendôme Palace.

The news gets worse and worse at home. Nobody knows how much snow there is now and the regular winds ensure that no communications are open. Those in town districts who have no fuel are advised to burn their furniture. The Home Secretary said, 'It is better to stay alive and be uncomfortable than die from cold.'

The air forces of France, Belgium, Germany and Holland are all flying supplies in and huge American planes have even dropped heating appliances and medical supplies at hospitals. There have been numerous air crashes and the American Air Force stated that its losses so far amount to seven helicopters and three aircraft of various types. It is rather odd I have not thought much of Edmund today, but I will before I go to sleep.

Thursday, 17 December. I again woke up for the six o'clock news. Apparently there were furious scenes in the Vendôme Palace. The leader of the opposition accused the Government of bringing countless deaths to the United Kingdom by accepting the deployment of cruise missiles: 'We were asking for trouble, and we got it. As for the future, surely the Prime Minister has a simple choice, to let the United States know that we shall not accept the deployment of Cruise Two missiles.'

Conservative Members, without exception, re-echoed the party line: the present crisis was terrible but to surrender would be to accept defeat. Surely that is right – we should wait a day or two to see whether any attention is being paid to the American proposal for talks with Russia.

The Labour Party, with one exception, wishes us to abandon cruise missiles, follow a policy of unilateral disarmament and speak to the Soviets from a position of moral strength.

Summing up, the Prime Minister spoke calmly, again emphasized sadly that the loss of life was calamitous, and extended all her sympathy to relatives of those who have died, but added that, 'in the long run, to stand firm and resolute will be better than giving in to blackmail, inspiring the Soviets to pick off the allies one by one. What is to stop the Soviet Union extending their cloud over countries and paralysing the whole West into submission?'

She was in close contact with the President of the United States and, while their conversations must of course remain private, she said she agreed wholeheartedly with every word of his broadcast, and informed the House that he will be broadcasting to the world again tomorrow morning at ten o'clock. Meanwhile she wished to praise the nation for its courage: 'Pain is often the price of victory and I believe that if Britain can survive by allied aid – which

I cannot praise enough – the USSR will understand that they cannot, by concealed brutality, wage a war of extinction without retribution.'

In America there have been further peace rallies and riots. The White House has been picketed, Jane Fonda and Rachel Ward lay down in front of the President's car. The television, at least in the south, works occasionally from new transmitters north of Paris. The gas and electricity is still coming through and London is still suffering much less than the country, where it is estimated that in the south of England there is no less than ten feet of level snow. No roads or railways are known to be open. Helicopter bases have been established in appalling conditions over the country by the Allied Air Forces. Our transport planes are now stationed in Holland, and with the help of the Americans are taking over the supply of the whole of the south of England. Other countries, France, Italy, etc., have all been allocated headquarters from which supplies are dropped on various areas and helicopter bases. Cold is still the main enemy. It is estimated that in hilly districts ninety per cent of all animals which are not under shelter have died. Scotland, Norway, Sweden and Finland are making contributions based on what is called their 'winter understanding' to help outlying districts. The islands are all cut off, but in view of the large supplies of food normally stocked, no especial fears are held.

I have not been asked to help in any way. The great difficulty is knowing what to do – reading is impossible. This diary helps, and I spring-clean the flat every day and try to teach the children sewing, but as I cannot sew I do not think they learn much. Their new friends, the boys, came up twice today and played cards which was a wonderful relief, and the relationship seems entirely innocent.

Once again, this time about six o'clock, there was a quiet, furtive sound of knocking. I was again afraid it was the detestable little Chase. But this time a nervous little woman with wispy grey hair and a pale freckled skin came skipping in directly I opened the door, as if she was being chased. She introduced herself as Mrs Stephens before I recognized her, and said we had never met because she and her husband never went out except on to their roof garden as he was confined to a bath chair and hated displaying his helplessness, but she had gone downstairs yesterday and later reported my words to him, and he had asked her to come and congratulate me on having spoken up against all this ridiculous communal eating. She had spoken to Mr Chase afterwards and made it quite plain she was not giving any of her food to him as she had to look after her husband. He eventually agreed, but he had not been a bit nice about it. She was worried about my girls, whom she had seen from her balcony. Were they having enough to eat? She had never had children herself, but as an ex-nurse she knew growing children required extra nourishment. I said they were all right and were playing cards with the boys from downstairs now.

She had seen them too, and added, 'Are they not quite a lot older?'

'Yes.'

'But still growing. Please all come along into my flat.'

It seemed a variation so I went and told the four children we had received an invitation. They looked absolutely blank but we all followed her. In her, or I should say his drawing room (she is so indefinite), which was well done in a conventional way with comfortable sofas and chairs, sat the husband with longish white hair, white skin and an aquiline nose. You could see he had been very good-looking. He spun the wheels round and came to meet us and said he was pleased to be able to thank me for having spoken sensibly yesterday. 'It is quite simple,' he said, 'the United States will have to make up their mind to take out this weather control station in Siberia or give in. I would guess that the Russians believe Europe will accept the abandonment of Cruise Two missiles rather than risk a nuclear war. But I would estimate the USA can destroy the plant by conventional weapons if they wish so there is a conventional warfare element which has not been considered. From how the President was speaking I would imagine he has some such action in mind and, even if casualties are high, it is a step away from nuclear war and would have the further advantage of putting the onus for a nuclear first strike on them. The President can also claim he has limited the conflict. Of course it could go wrong. If we are all destroyed I will personally be pleased to be blown out of this damn chair. But I will be sad for all you young people.'

'Oh Howard,' his wife said, 'what things you do say. You young things come this way.'

They followed her and I was left with the bitter Mr Stephens, who looked at me curiously, and said, 'I am interested in the effect crisis has on individuals. Tell me, in this, what must be the most frightening time of your life, are you thinking of yourself or of your children?'

I said, 'I honestly do not know. I am certain that in a quick emergency like a shipwreck or a fire I would think of them first, but in this imprisonment which goes on and on I am not sure that I do not, despite all my attempts, think mostly of myself, although of course I would willingly die for them.'

'I thought so,' he said, looking pleased.

His attitude annoyed me and we did not speak again until the door opened and Mrs Stephens came in, followed by the boys and girls. They each had a tin of Huntley and Palmers biscuits in one hand and a pot of jam in the other, and appeared to be on the verge of bursting into fits of laughter. I quickly stood up and thanked her and said how pleased I was to meet him.

He held my hand for an embarrassingly long time and when he let it go said, with a hint of the pathetic in his voice, 'Please come and see me again. I did not think anyone had any intelligence in the whole place.'

Directly Mrs Stephens closed the door, the children exploded and I had to push them into the flat in case she heard. Apparently she insisted on giving them all a spoonful of some sort of sticky malt and, despite the boys refusing, had thrust it into their mouths, then she got out from an enormous store cupboard tins of biscuits and jam and told them to come back whenever they were hungry. Lucy said she was going again in the morning, it was so funny, but the boys said she could go alone. Well, it was a diversion.

On the late night news nothing new except a blast of propaganda from the Soviets denying they were responsible for the snowfall.

Afterwards a flat statement, to the effect that positive military action would be considered an act of aggression, and result in an equivalent response. Well; there we are, we will know if we are going to die in a day or two. I think it would probably be nicer to be killed by nuclear missiles than slowly die in this place.

Friday, 18 December. Still snowing. Thirteen feet of level snow. I woke up at eight o'clock this morning which was marvellous as the early hours, when I just lie, are desperate. As I prepared breakfast I could not help thinking of my spontaneous reply to Mr Stephens. Am I thinking more of myself? Do I think less about Edmund? As for William, I can honestly say I have not given him a thought. And as Lucy and Anne have only once shown any signs of fear and do not even realize what is happening, I have not felt needed. Of course it is frightful to think of their young lives ending, but honestly I cannot think about them either, although, as I have already written, I would willingly die for them. I know I shall love Edmund when or if I see him again, but he now seems to belong to another world of long ago, and I find myself thinking more and more about my own past and even of Mr Stephens.

Somehow I, them, all of us, seem unimportant, but still I think of myself. After all, to die is a personal experience! I remember quite seriously wondering yesterday what my mother had given me for my seventh birthday that I loathed so much and burnt. I was really annoyed at not remembering. I do not know if everyone else is like this or just myself, and if the reason I am not afraid is because I am suffering from shock, or simply that I realize my absolute irrelevance.

Saturday, 19 December. The day's news began with reports of further demonstrations in America and a statement from the White House that the President will make a further statement tomorrow morning at nine a.m., three p.m. our time. We had breakfast and then there was a knock on the door and one of the Thompson boys came in. I thought it was a bit much if they were starting to call at nine o'clock, but he was very pale and said he had come to tell us that Chase, believing the snow would be harder at night, had gone out on his skis to see if the main street was open and had not returned. Nobody had any idea what to do. There had been some talk of a rescue party, but as it was not known where he had gone it seemed a waste of time. The Thompson boy said his wife was taking his loss bravely, and I could not help thinking that perhaps she was secretly pleased. But why do I hate him, I only saw him twice. His plan was silly, but surely I cannot hate him for such a little thing and feel positively glad he is missing. Am I getting odd?

The debate in the House of Commons continued yesterday and there is also growing unease in France that the Russians may extend their snow belt, I suppose to put pressure on us to give in. As they do not intend to accept the Cruise Two missiles they have made 'firm and continuous' protests in Moscow but have received the same deadpan answer: 'The Soviet Government is not responsible for the weather.'

I don't know why, but about midday I went and knocked on Mr Stephens' door to talk to him. It was a wonderful relief to speak to an intelligent man. He told me his history. He had been in the Foreign Office before breaking his back seven years ago in a car accident. He avoided his friends afterwards as he sensed their pity, which he found unbearable. Subsequently he married his nurse, not out of affection, but because she was so silly, she could not understand anything except looking after him. During these past years he had lived by reading and writing.

I asked him what he had written and he said, 'Nothing good enough to show you yet, but I have burned three books. Each of them was better than the one before. I am determined to do something very good and, as I have all the time in the world and never see anybody except my two sisters who are almost as stupid as my wife, I have no possible excuse. I have found these last days very exciting, but when I saw you yesterday it made me wonder whether I have not made a mistake and should have lived among people, pity and all! Anyhow, please come back and see me every day. This may not be a demanding request – we may live for only three or four.'

On going back to my flat I sat down and thought about Mr Stephens. I think I shall always think of him as Mr Stephens. A Christian name would not suit him. Today I noticed his eyes for the first time; I think he cannot have looked at me before. They change with rapidity, expressing pleasure, impatience or anger.

His face is birdlike in that the nose is the dominating feature. And the rest, as it were, slopes away. But he is still good-looking although his lips are thin. I am sure this is the result of a hermit existence. They do not look natural.

Later in the afternoon there was enormous excitement. A helicopter came swinging over the house and dropped a square wooden box on my roof garden. Everyone came piling through my door as if they were Robinson Crusoes. It was ridiculous. They all have plenty of food and I should not think the contents will be touched, in fact I think some people might rather die than eat them. There were hundreds of bars of black chocolate and a sack of flour and fifty little cases entitled 'iron rations' which nobody opened; that was all. There was universal disappointment and people looked so sad I offered them a drink and gave them some of the red wine I was going to have at dinner. At once everyone started being nice to me and saying communal eating was a ridiculous idea of Chase's and more and more of them had been taking meals in their rooms. And now he has disappeared anybody can collect their little labelled stores. I will send the girls down tomorrow.

Well, we drank about twelve bottles of wine. I even gave Lucy and the boys some. Getting drunk made me feel more cheerful and we all laughed getting dinner ready and I went to bed without a care in the world, or even bothering to listen to the late night news.

Sunday, 20 December. There are now at least fifteen and a half feet of level snow everywhere, and goodness knows how long it will take to clear away or what the floods will be like! The Government, looking on the bright side, have told people living in certain areas, such as the Vale of York and the Thames Valley, to start moving furniture into their upper floors as when the thaw comes the floods may be uncontrollable. It must be comforting to know that if you are not going to be snowed to death you will be drowned!

Since the party a spirit of camaraderie has been established, and several people looked in to see me. The one topic of conversation is what the President is going to say. Will he give in or will he risk a nuclear war on our behalf? The same old argument goes backwards and forwards; if he gives in to blackmail the USA could be next. But it seems to me that America is a long way away from England and a lot of Americans do not like the English, and a lot of Americans will let the President know they do not want a nuclear war because of us. Anyhow, we can only wait helplessly.

The President spoke slowly, posing as an efficient, down-to-earth man in the street. He said he was not going to use any technical jargon but was just going to say how he saw things, and how he saw things was that a deliberate attempt was being made to destroy a nation by 'a perversion of nature'. He was convinced, and his advisers were convinced, although he knew there were those who disagreed, that the United States could not condone such a method of warfare without coming to the defence of allies to whom they were ethically committed. He had ascertained and subsequently confirmed that the causes of the present snowfall on Britain emanated from northern Siberia, an area scarcely populated by man, but known in recent years to have been the scene of continuous experimentation. Taking into consideration all satellite photographs, it was apparent that the snowfall originated in a hundred-square-mile area in the Severnaya Zemlya group of so-called islands just south of the Arctic Circle: 'Our experts inform us that the Soviet Union could continue to produce snow there in Arctic conditions and wind-direct it to desired locations until the United Kingdom is as dead as John Brown. This the United States cannot permit.'

Now there was a lot of talk about him having his finger on the nuclear trigger. But there were other triggers than nuclear triggers and he was the last man to want to put the Soviet Union in a position where it was forced to retaliate by nuclear warfare.

On the other hand the suffocation of an ally could not be allowed to proceed unhindered. He had therefore ordered the mobilization of all conventional armed forces and, some time after two a.m. tomorrow, unless the Soviet President agreed to discuss the future with him and end the snowfall, 'conventional methods, and I repeat the word "conventional", will be used to nullify the relevant area'.

The USA was not attacking but retaliating. 'We may well suffer grievous losses, but losses are always suffered in war, and what we are doing, I reiterate, is taking a military step, not a nuclear initiative. If it fails we will have to plan otherwise. I hope the nation will support me. The decision is difficult, our dedication to peace is absolute. I pray God the outcome will be successful.'

Nobody knows what to make of his speech, having presumed an attack by either side would automatically start a nuclear war. In the evening I gave another drinks party. I discovered that William had over twenty cases of wine in a cupboard in his room so we should be able to have a party every night. When we were all quite merry we turned on the news and heard the Prime Minister appealing to the Soviets to cease their interference with the weather and agree to talks. The number of Cruise Two missiles to be deployed in the United Kingdom would be reduced if Soviet missiles were correspondingly reduced. The Labour Party concentrated on the dangers of starting a nuclear war, and old Mr Foot said we were progressing inexorably to war, slipping downhill to death at an ever-increasing pace 'like a stone rolling too fast to gather moss'.

A late-night commentator said 'Severnaya Zemlya' means 'North Lands'. Who cares!

Monday, 21 December. About nineteen feet now, and still precisely two hours of steady winds each day. The hospitals appear to be managing, thanks to the American air-drops, but the death-rate among old people is thought to be enormous. Also, large numbers of children seem to have disappeared, unable to resist sliding out of first-floor windows to play in the snow. How horrifying, yet how quickly one becomes tough.

We still have five hours to wait before the President's twenty-four-hour limit is up, when I suppose they will make a conventional missile or bombing raid, perhaps somewhere here! Neutral estimates suggest the Russians were taken aback by the President's initiative and there may not be large-scale maintenance facilities for defence fighters in the Siberian region.

Mrs Chase – a very nice girl – and not looking unhappy (so perhaps I was instinctively right about him) came for some of the helicopter flour. I gave her several tins and told her to come for Christmas lunch. She burst into tears.

Two o'clock came and nothing happened and we were all glued to the wireless at three and four. My now nightly party started at six, still without news. At ten o'clock there was nothing so we had a merry evening and Mr Stephens allowed himself to be wheeled in and said that now he was no longer as certain he was going to die as he was last week.

Tuesday, 22 December. I woke up at five o'clock in my fear of missing the six o'clock news. Still nothing, and so it went on all through the morning until eleven o'clock – six o'clock American time – when it was announced that, after forty hours of clear warning to the Soviet Union a number of American bombers of the secret 'Jupiter Force' had dropped from an undisclosed height a large number of high explosives on an unnamed Siberian site. All planes were now, without loss, over two thousand miles away from the target area.

But it is still snowing. There was no further statement from America, except to the effect that every eventuality had been considered and prepared for. At half past five it was rumoured the Soviet Union had informed the President that its national sovereignty had been violated and that a conventional air-attack constituted an act of war. However, there was no talk of war being declared, and once again the pundits took every point of view, one military expert saying the 'Jupiter Force' can fly at two hundred thousand feet and bomb with pin-point accuracy.

I had forgotten Europe. Somehow it does not seem to count, but every NATO country is now mobilized. Here, of course, no one can do anything. According to the wireless there are protests everywhere against the Americans, mixed with vociferous support. But the protesters sound rather frightened which makes me wonder whether fear was the reason for their protests. I think the trouble is that idealists are both the best and the worst people.

The children asked about the news and said wasn't the American action pointless if it did not stop snowing? This was about six p.m. I said yes, peered out of the window and it had stopped, but goodness knows how much is on the ground now – well over twenty feet.

All at once there was a hubbub in the passage and some of my new so-called friends had come to say how wonderfully 'the American bombing' had succeeded. Just after, we heard the weather man talking in a superior way about a general diffusion of the clouds and reports of light snow spreading across east Ireland and central France.

Afterwards I went to see Mr Stephens. He was concise: 'They will have to retaliate and your and our future depends on how. Perhaps their wisest course would be to drop conventional bombs on the United Kingdom to show that it is within their capability to destroy us and encourage our allies to think the snow war can be confined. They will not fire missiles at Europe, they will respond to limited force by limited force. The alternative to a European attack could be a conventional attack on the United States, enough to satisfy their pride. It remains to be seen whether the American reaction will be tough or fearful. But for goodness sake do not repeat what I have said – I do not want all those dreadful women coming screaming in here asking my opinion.'

I went back quietly to my room and asked the children what they would like for supper – they said hamburgers with cheese and an egg on them. I made four and gave them some of the last bottles of Coca Cola and told them to invite the two young Thompson boys. Then I went and tried to read in my room and heard them laughing and talking for a long time. How strange it is that the young should overcome the insurmountable barriers of age when they are in danger. I suppose they will stop being friends if peace comes and the boys realize they can see girls of their own age. I kept the wireless low while I read, to hear if anything had happened. It went droning on about protests in Europe and America.

At ten-thirteen p.m. – I am writing this at ten-fifteen – it was announced that Soviet aircraft have attacked Alaska. First reports suggested a large number of planes have been shot down and little damage done. The Pentagon is to issue a statement in half an hour.

Once again the whole crowd came piling into my flat. It may seem odd but I cannot differentiate between them. The men all appear old and fatuous; the women unbearable. But when I am drunk they suddenly turn into bearable nondescripts, like relations. I got out more red wine but this time there was desperation in the air. I noticed that those already drunk when they came drank more, but became no drunker.

At eleven o'clock there was a United States Government communication tersely stating in language I cannot repeat that approximately two hundred unidentified aircraft had attacked Alaskan oilfields. At least four had been shot down. The extent of the damage could not yet be assessed. Then the commentators had a field day. Some said it meant nuclear war, some not. The general inclination was to blame the President. Everyone left at once and I took two sleeping pills.

Wednesday, 23 December. I slept intermittently and badly and my thoughts so worried me that I went across the passage to see Mr Stephens in his bedroom before breakfast. Although it was only seven o'clock he was already in his wheelchair. Mrs Stephens started fluttering round as usual but I was brusque and said I wanted to talk to him about something serious which made her immediately fade away, looking worried. I told him of my fears, which had been increased by his curiosity, and how I believed my selfish character was beginning to let me down, causing obsession with myself and carelessness of my children. It really worried me because I knew I loved them, always had and always would, and would certainly sacrifice my life for them, but in my secret heart I was now becoming indifferent to them. Compared to the whole tragedy of millions of deaths they somehow seemed irrelevant, unimportant. Was I wicked?

He wheeled over to me, put his hand on my arm and said, 'No, you are not being wicked, you are being honest, and you cannot be good unless you are honest. But why worry? If things blow up in a day or two God will have so many millions of people to think about He will not have time to bother about an honest thought of yours; if, on the other hand, war is averted you will find you love the children in exactly the same way as you did before. You will cease to depend on me as you do now, and you will again be in love with whoever you were in love with. Things will go back to normal for you. Not alas for me.' And he wheeled away.

It shows how selfish I am that I felt rather relieved, left immediately, and was as nice as I could be to the children, but they seemed so normal and unconcerned, it appears unnecessary to have bothered.

Thursday, 24 December. The news claimed that immense damage has been caused in Alaska. An oil terminal has been destroyed and a vast amount of stored oil is on fire. The United States was said to be considering its position. There is nothing to do but wait and pray. I did not bother to ask the children what they wanted for lunch or even to start getting it, but I longed to do something. So I went in and kissed Mr Stephens on the lips. Neither of us spoke a word.

Afterwards I went downstairs and asked if anyone was ill or needed help. The whole communal life has collapsed and everybody has gone back with their own food to their own apartments and avoids poor pretty Mrs Chase. But you meet people walking around as if in a hospital. I felt desperate and could not live through such another morning. Then the White House announced the President would again speak to the world. Nobody dared guess what he was going to say. I ate no lunch, but told the children to get theirs. They opened some of the iron rations and said they tasted of iron. I did not even smile.

At four p.m. our time the President spoke. I should not think anyone has ever been listened to by so many people before. He said that the United States had never desired war, but refused to see its allies subdued by new and horrendous methods which could not be disguised as natural phenomena. He had therefore, with reluctance, ordered a strike by the nation's secret force of new high-level bombers:

'This was in every sense successful. The planes flew at a height which should not be discussed and perhaps would not be believed. They achieved their objective, and they returned to base without loss.'

He regretted having to announce that the USSR Air Force had been ordered to retaliate as if the United States were the aggressor. As a result, considerable destruction had been wrought in Alaska; American soil had been bombed and as yet unknown casualties sustained, whose names would be announced later; oil refineries and terminals had been severely damaged. He asked himself was this senseless war to continue? Last night on his own initiative he had communicated with the President of the Soviet Union and told him he had no alternative but to give him a twelve-hour ultimatum: either the two Presidents should meet at an agreed site to discuss the general reduction of missile weapons in Europe or hostilities would be resumed. He said he had pointed out to the Soviet Union that the assault on the American homeland would not or could not be tolerated by the nation and, if by eight a.m. Washington time Tuesday (two hours ago), he had not received an affirmative reply from the Soviet leader, retaliation, which could lead to total warfare, would be made by the United States. He had afterwards gone through with God's aid what he described as the longest sleepless hours of his life. Two and a half hours ago the President of the USSR telephoned and agreed to a meeting while maintaining all defence and retaliatory capabilities.

'The United States therefore at present plans no further military action. A meeting on neutral ground is to take place within the next two weeks. I would like to thank God that the firm courage shown by the citizens of our country has averted war.'

It seemed too good to be true. I rushed in to see Mr Stephens. I have never even asked his Christian name. He seemed the only person who understood the double talk that goes on. What did it mean, I asked him.

'It means there will be no nuclear war. It means it will start thawing in England and a lot of people will be drowned and killed in the floods. It means probably for a good number of years there will not be another nuclear confrontation. It means the USA is lucky to have a possession like Alaska, detached from the national pride and conscience. It means there will be a temporary reduction of missiles on both sides. It means I will have to go on living in this damned chair and I hope it means that you will continue to be a friend.'

I kissed him on the lips again as Mrs Stephens came in and dropped a tray but I did not care, and gave her a kiss too on the way out, and went straight back to my flat and kissed the children for about five minutes and told them everything was all right.

They seemed puzzled and said, 'You always said it would be, Mummy.'

I could only laugh, but stopped quickly. I remembered it was Christmas tomorrow and I had before me the task of decorating the horrid little tree. But then it is wonderful to have something like this to worry about. Now it is all over I am going to break every resolution I made about keeping a diary because I blame myself for the whole thing. Everything seems to have blown up because of my decision. I fear if I write another word it may start all over again.

At the same time the Prime Minister of England was telephoned by the President of the United States.

'Hello, Prime Minister, I thought . . .'

'Mr President, I would like to thank you for your wonderful support and bravery. Without your courage we might all have been destroyed.'

'Thank you, Prime Minister. I appreciate that it has been a tough time but I never believed they wanted a nuclear war. The trouble was they realized correctly that we did not either, so we had to play-act, pretend we were ready for anything. As a matter of fact, I am not sure we could not have gone on bombing each other in Siberia and Alaska for a long time before things got hot. But we had a problem. Our raid on the snow producers was one hundred per cent successful, while their retaliation in Alaska was a one hundred per cent disaster. They had not got the height our planes had. Our missiles alone downed thirty-six and they never hit a thing except maybe a few goddam reindeer.

'My boys came in all set to announce another great victory, but here I would like to say I owe a mighty big debt to old Henry Kress who was in my office at the time.

'He said, "Hold it, get the CIA to close the whole area for clearance of unexploded bombs then go in, blow up a terminal, a couple of depots and the smallest refinery. Get every photographer up there, send the photographs round the world, make the Russians pretend they hit us hard. Do not state their real air losses, only ours. They will be grateful. If we show they failed all round they might do something damned silly. We have been indecently successful."

'Well, I took his advice and it worked, but keep it quiet, will you?'

She said she would.

Charlotte Gwynne

The following story relates to a period of social history which existed for a few years at the end of the Second World War. In it the debutante system staggered to its feet, staggered and mercifully succumbed to a timely death.

Before the War an aristocratic young girl's life ran along ordered lines. She had a nanny, a governess, followed nearly always by a few years of select schooling concluded by a visit of several months to a 'finishing' academy in Paris or Florence. During holidays she lived or frequently stayed in large houses where she came to know her relations and her parents' friends and children. The rites culminated in a presentation at Court and a season of parties, race-meetings and weekends. For original, shy or clever girls the process was torture; socially graded, they had to sit next to the same fatuous young men with whom they had nothing in common at party after party. On the other hand, to the silly, pretty girl it was the promised land to which, alas, she could never afterwards return. But to one and all it was an ordered life in which their fate was controlled by others.

In the limbo years of the post-war era, everything changed. With few exceptions, the great houses were closed or run down; governesses were almost unknown; Florence and Paris were out of the question. The educational problem was frequently solved by the use of local schools. Girls ceased to meet their relations and were confined by petrol rationing to a restricted area. In short, those educated at this time became provincial and led narrow, sheltered lives which retarded their development and encouraged their eccentricities. Moreover, the mundane security of their lives collapsed when – with only the prelude of one or two embarrassing 'young people's' dances at which spotty boys stood on their toes – they were finally thrown, insecure and unprepared, into an adult world. Women's service in the war and their increasing demands for equality had destroyed the law of manners. Thus once again it was torture to original, shy or clever girls, because young men no longer found it socially necessary to be polite, dance, talk or sit next to them. Unless they conformed they were in danger of sitting alone.

The heroine of this anecdote should be conceived as one born with every conceivable advantage, but who was momentarily plagued by shyness and uncertainty in a confused and uncertain epoch.

The door banged open. Charlotte Gwynne sat up half awake, and made out against the background of a dimly lit passage the figure of a maid with tousled hair peering into the room. She reached to turn on the light and the door was immediately pulled shut. Looking around in amazement at the dingy wallpaper with its pattern of chrysanthemums rubbed bare and spotted with stains, at the thin, faded curtains hanging unevenly from chipped wooden rings and the little square of carpet isolated on the cracked linoleum, she wondered where she was. The events of yesterday came slowly back – the late arrival in Perth, the search for a cheap place, the recommendation of a temperance hotel, the climb to a dingy room on the second floor, a last request to be called early to catch the train. In sudden panic she reached out impulsively for her alarm clock and knocked on the floor a tooth-glass of water. In relief she lay back. She had plenty of time.

But soon, uneasiness defeating sleep, she dressed quickly, balancing with difficulty on the little square of carpet. Then with a guilty feeling she mopped up the spilt water, meticulously searching for every sliver of broken glass and stacking them in a neat pile on the bedside table. Closing her suitcase, she walked on tiptoe downstairs and knocked uncertainly several times on an internal window before the manager, unshaved, his hair standing up, pulling on a grey dressing-gown, reluctantly jerked it open. She asked for the bill, to which he must add the price of the broken tooth-glass. He gave her a surprised look and put down one extra shilling, reflected, and slowly turned the one into a two. She did not object, rather was relieved he had not complained. She paid from her dwindling little roll of pound notes and politely asked the way to the station. Luckily, the answer was simple:

'Right out of the door, second turn left, second turn right, and it's in front of you.'

Thanking him with a profuseness which made him shake his head in disbelief before banging the window shut, she left the hotel repeating to herself again and again the instructions, until she found to her relief that they had brought her to her destination.

She relaxed for the first time that morning and looked about her at the ugly station and the sky, clear, unclouded, promising a fine day. This made her feel that there could be something nice about Perth. Entering the empty echoing station she bought a third-class ticket and sat down to wait. For the second time that morning she suffered a sudden fright. Her watch showed six-fifteen, but it was the gift of an unreliable friend of her mother's. Was it unreliable itself? Had the train come and gone? With fumbling fingers she opened her suitcase – her alarm clock confirmed her watch – but she was not entirely satisfied until she checked with the station clock too.

The train, when it arrived, was empty. Contented, she took out her novel by Trollope – a new discovery – and immediately lost herself in a world indifferent to stops and starts. Her peace was ended by a porter opening her carriage door, shouting: 'All out, Glasgow!' Alarmed that the train was starting back immediately for Perth, she jumped out in such haste that only his arm prevented her from falling. She started to thank him in a dignified manner, but remembering her book on the carriage seat had to climb in and out again before finishing her sentence.

She was reassured to find that the Douglastown train left in two hours. She went into the hotel to have coffee, bacon and eggs, and while she ate determined to avoid the mistakes of which she had nearly always been guilty on the rare occasions she had travelled alone, taking the wrong train or by-passing her destination. She rechecked that Rowanhill was the fourth stop. It was, and the train was waiting in the station. Soon she was once again sitting in a corner seat of a third-class carriage reading her book. But when the train started she put it away and looked out at the murky suburbs and dirty countryside. At a place called Fellmarnock the door opened and in came a red-haired man wearing a flat cap which lay like a plate on his head. With deliberation he placed his bag on the rack, his cap on the next seat, sat down opposite her and opened a newspaper which he fully extended so that the printed page must almost have touched the end of his nose. Below the paper she could see that his coat had two enormous pockets, lying like gamebags above trousers round without the pretence of a crease, and huge boots laced up to the ankle. All this was reassuring; if not a farmer he was surely associated with the farming community and a blood brother to her father's tenants.

Secure that she could rely on him to say when they neared her destination she happily returned to her book until a remark of Mrs Proudie's made her laugh and lift her head. Looking down again she saw with dismay the number of the page. Had she read so much? Could she have passed her destination? To ease her mind, she decided to ask the man opposite where they were. But it was not easy. On this, her first independent journey, commands of her upbringing still unconsciously dominated her behaviour. She had been frequently told it was bad manners not to look into the eyes of those to whom you spoke. But how? All she could see of the red-haired man opposite were red finger-ends. There appeared no alternative to rudeness so she bravely addressed the newspaper:

'Could you please tell me if we have passed Rowanhill?'

The paper was slowly lowered, still held to its full extent, and a pair of green eyes examined her over the paper top, then he said in a rough, kind voice:

'You're reeght, lassie,' and the paper covered his eyes again.

At first, she was reassured, second thoughts caused doubt. Could he have said 'you are right' meaning the train had passed Rowanhill? Desperately she wished she had phrased the question better. But the train was beginning to slow down. If it had gone too far she must get out at once. Again, she plucked up her courage: 'Please, I'm rather deaf,' she lied desperately, 'is this station we're coming to before or after Rowanhill?'

Again he lowered his newspaper.

'Sanquhat,' he said slowly.

'Sanquhat?' she repeated out loud in amazement, thinking to herself, surely that's an Indian name.

'Aye, Sanquhat,' he said, jerking his paper with both hands sideways towards the platform, where large letters confirmed his statement.

'Thank you,' she said feebly, beginning to wonder if she had belatedly achieved a childish dream of passing like Alice through the looking glass. Fortunately, her thoughts communicated themselves to him. After an intense stare, out came the magic words:

'Rowanhill next stop.'

When they arrived, she thanked him and they smiled at each other as she descended from the carriage in a very dignified way, not forgetting her book this time. He closed the door and smiled again through the window. For some reason she felt happy. Giving in her ticket, she looked once again at the station clock and saw that everything was going according to plan. She had an hour before the car was coming to fetch her. Sitting down on a railway bench she again opened her book, but could no longer concentrate. The shadows of the coming visit hovered too near to be dismissed. She must not panic, she had no reason to be shy or consider herself a failure, but she knew that unless she somehow reassured herself she would lose confidence and say and do silly things.

She had two methods of reassurance and decided to try the first, which was based on complete honesty and for that reason did not always work. It was an exact definition of her position. She opened her suitcase, took out a black-sheeted notebook and wrote:

1. 'I am pretty.' Immediately it occurred to her that perhaps this was not true. She took a little round mirror out of her bag and stared at herself critically. Her hair was untidy so she combed it, looked again, and decided that although she was not conceited, she was nevertheless undeniably pretty, thin, with long arms and legs, dark hair and beautiful hands. The statement could stand.

2. 'I am clever; although again I find this difficult to believe.'

3. 'My Scottish visits have all been a success, I think people have liked me and, apart from difficulties in finding bathrooms and constantly walking into strangers' bedrooms, I have made no mistakes.'

4. 'My fear of strangers is irrational, and Eleanor is both a cousin and a friend.'

5. 'If I give in to my fears, I shall be a failure.'

6. 'I am determined not to be a failure, but as I am pretty and clever there is no reason why I should be.'

Reassured, she put the list carefully into a bag, but before long her doubts returned. There only remained her second method, the resorting to what she secretly called her 'confidence book'. As it lay at the bottom of her suitcase, its extraction necessitated the unpacking and placing on the station seat of her evening dresses and other clothes. Unaware of the amazement felt by local travellers at the sight of a dazzlingly pretty girl sitting on a bench, looking at a book, surrounded by clothes not often publicly exhibited in Scotland in those days, she read the first cutting (the book was a collection of cuttings). It dated from two years before and read: 'Also at this party for the younger set was the Marchioness of Stourminster, accompanied by her daughter, Lady Charlotte Gwynne, who certainly continues the family tradition of great beauty.'

There followed a number of similarly phrased compliments which she now knew by heart and to which she gave scant attention. But, after a few pages, she stopped and carefully examined a full-length photograph of herself, her eyes huge, her face heart-shaped, in a long white dress swathed with tulle. She supposed she did look beautiful – although it was rather a pity it did not show her eyes were blue – but take away the tulle and the lilies and was she? She could never get over the photographs of her mother's friends by Cecil Beaton. Friends she considered plain, yet transformed by him into beauties. With a little sigh she turned over another page to read a cutting surrounded by a red pencil:

'As is usual this season, onc of the focal points was Lady Charlotte Gwynne, as always the centre of laughter and gaiety.'

She remembered the evening well and hoped the report was true. Certainly she had danced the whole evening and two of the young men had asked her to marry them. She was not in the least concerned to hear later that one was considered a lunatic. He had been part of a pleasant evening and she was grateful to him. But to be honest – and she was determined, whatever she might say in public, to be truthful with herself in private – she had not been a great social success so far, having spent too large a proportion of too many balls in ladies' cloakrooms to make that claim.

The whole thing was puzzling, for a lot of the girls who were greater successes seemed idiotic gigglers to her, and the same could be said about most of the young men she sat next to. Without any conceit she knew that she was cleverer, and was not prepared to sink to their level. Her dilemma was, she supposed, that she wanted them to like and admire her when she was not prepared to say and do the sort of things which would make them. And if this was the case why did she want them to like her? Was it because she wanted to belong to the world of her mother and father whose friends, even if stupid, seemed to have a unity of feeling and width of view which caused their faults to be forgotten; while the nicest of them were so very nice.

Lately at the back of her mind had been a dream – certainly not more than a dream – of marrying a young man she had met and danced with and, far more important, had talked to twice with a wonderful utter abandonment of shyness and uneasiness. He was incredibly good-looking, attractive, funny, clever, one day to be the possessor of every worldly advantage, but indissolubly linked with success. To marry him would be perfect, but she could not possibly do it without living and being a success in his world. And she also had to admit that when she stayed with the parents of those her parents called her 'middle-class friends' she felt ill at ease. Little things they said or did – which there was no reason why they should not say or do – embarrassed her and made her feel awkward for them. It was all so difficult. Was she a snob?

At any rate, all she knew at the moment was that she was determined to be a success with the people among whom she had been brought up. This admitted and decided, she had then to admit to feeling considerable fear over the prospect of the next ten days, to be spent with her cousin and his wife Mary, terrifying, beautiful, who certainly did not suffer fools gladly. She reopened her 'confidence book' and read:

'Without doubt, the most beautiful and charming of this year's vintage is Lady Charlotte Gwynne, which is not surprising, considering that she is Lady Stourminster's daughter.'

She wished they would leave her mother out of it and, repeating to herself three times the first part of the sentence, decided that she was at least as presentable as anybody else. Feeling much better, she shut the book and repacked it at the bottom of her case, realizing with dismay that her underclothes and dressing-gown were draped over the station seat. Blushing and not daring to see if anybody was staring, she quickly repacked, powdered her nose and sat with her eyes down-cast waiting for the car.

Her first sight of Castlerowan standing pink, upright, castellated on a little hill, reassured her. It was certainly magnificent, built in pale pink stone with elaborate carved windows and in its centre a curving double staircase; but she was relieved to feel a snobbish pleasure, recognized and admitted: it was certainly not as magnificent as Gwynne. A butler led her on to the lawn at the other side of the house, where a frightening number of people sat on deck-chairs and cushions. She looked around in confusion and was pleased to recognize and be recognized by her host and cousin William, who explained that his wife, Mary, would be back for dinner. He shook hands but did not seem pleased to see her and quickly shouted for his daughter, her so-called friend Eleanor, who was in the house, to introduce her to everybody. She was never quite sure whether or not they liked each other, but as all the last year they had gone to the same house-parties, race-meetings and dances, she supposed they must.

They went and sat with Eleanor's brother Henry and his friends. Charlotte had seen him several times, but could not remember him ever having said anything to her but 'good evening'. He had two friends with him. All three had red hair. It made her think of Sherlock Holmes and the red-haired league, and she thought of making a joke but stopped herself quickly, remembering recent painful discoveries that outside her own home to make literary references, let alone jokes, was a very risky business, checking conversation and calling for explanations which, when haltingly given, were listened to in a polite embarrassed silence, as if excusing bad taste. This constraint was irritating, as it would have been a funny joke; at Gwynne it would have been taken up, exaggerated, but not here, she realized. This was not a good omen, she would always have to think what she should say. Uneasiness always made her look stupid.

She sat silently, on her best behaviour, watching. The cleverest of the party was an animated young man of twenty-five, Mark Cartwright, a slight acquaintance, one of Eleanor's admirers, lean, green, clever, ugly. He divided his time making up to her and twisting his face into agreeable grimaces in attempts to please the older generation of shooting men. Her fears came back. She could never think of anything to say about shooting; perhaps a drink would change her outlook. She paused; a drink often caused her to say stupid things. Anyway, the danger was not very great. The only drink she could see on a silver salver was a bottle of South African sherry, surrounded by a group of very small glasses; nobody offered her one anyway.

At lunch, she was placed next to one of the red-heads and cousin William who, she hoped, would not ask her about her father's farming experiments. Desperately she tried to remember what they were. Sure enough, he immediately turned and, having asked whether the grouse were scarce further north and hearing with apparent pleasure that they were, went on: 'I hear your father is experimenting a lot.'

'Oh yes,' she said brightly, as if she were continuously involved with them.

Cousin William seemed somewhat displeased and looked her up and down, as if he was considering whether or not to say something unpleasant. The idea occurred to her for the first time that these experiments, of which she had heard so much in total incomprehension, could be inhumane, in which case she would have to defend her father. But if so, her complete ignorance of the subject made it likely she would do so badly. She began to be furious with herself. Why was she so incurious? Unexpectedly, cousin William came to her aid with what seemed at first sight an innocuous question.

'How many acres are there at Gwynne?'

'A hundred thousand,' she said without thinking.

'A hundred thousand? Are you quite sure? And how much is down to forestry?'

'A quarter, I think,' she said wildly.

'A quarter? Do you mean to say he has twenty-five thousand acres of woodland?'

His voice was full of incomprehensible anger. Charlotte had not yet understood the jealousy of the great landlords.

'And do you mean he employs two hundred and fifty foresters? For with the high rainfall in the West Country you could not plant, clean and prune with less than a man per hundred acres? Or can you? Or do you?'

Charlotte now felt like a discredited witness. She had no idea of the number of her father's acres, or of his employees. All she could say was, as she tossed her head in distress:

'Oh dear, I'm so bad at figures, I am sure I am wrong.'

Cousin William seemed to cheer up a little.

'Well, yes, I think you may be. Anyhow, I will write and ask Tommy. I want to speak in the next session in the Lords' on increasing grants for forestry. If he has such big interests he should support me.'

With the satisfied movement of one who has proved a point, he turned away, leaving Charlotte aghast: her father would be furious, he never understood her inability to master mathematics or figures. Oh dear, everything was going wrong.

The afternoon was not so bad. She sat in her room and wrote thank-you letters to the hostesses of her Northern tour. Two had to be rewritten as it was obviously tactless to write: 'Castlerowan is the prettiest house in the prettiest place in Scotland' as she had noticed every landowner in Scotland either thought he had the prettiest house or, if that was impossible, the prettiest view. Her task finished, she went and looked out of the window – the lawn was empty – she crept downstairs and out of the side entrance for what her mother called 'one of your sleep-walks', in which they told her she would be seen bending silent, intent, with a wild flower held gently in her hand, or standing motionless with her head pressed to the bark of a huge beech or oak. She never bothered to remember where she had been, what she had thought, refusing to be on the defensive. All she knew was she loved the peace and loneliness of woods, they calmed her, reduced her worries. Today she sat on a bank and looked down at a stream for a timeless period, but was back in her room in plenty of time to change for dinner. Eleanor came in, was very friendly, said they had all missed her, had she everything she wanted? Did she know where the bathroom was? As she was going out, she stopped and said, over her shoulder:

'Oh, by the way, Mummy told me to tell you she's had to put you next to Baba Peebles at dinner.'

At once, Charlotte's nerves started fluttering. She had no idea who Baba Peebles was and now, obviously, it was stupid to ask. She remembered hearing the name Baba spoken before lunch on the lawn: but as nobody ever answered, she had thought he or she must be the little whippet which had sat shivering under a bamboo chair. Surely she could not be sitting next to a dog at dinner? No, not here. The name must represent a frightening person, but she could not think who. Neither did she dare ask as she sipped her glass of sherry before dinner when, noticing an uneasy feeling of intrusion, she looked round and found her cousin Mary, whom she had not seen for years, staring at her with an interest so intense she could only toss her head in a hopeless attempt to hide. Distinctly across the room floated the comment:

'Yes; very pretty, but like a foal standing up for the first time,' spoken so quickly the words ran into each other. To complete her confusion Eleanor chose that moment to come up to take her over to her mother. The same voice said: 'Oh; I have just been saying you're even more beautiful than your mother.'

The beautiful mouth smiled then the eyes looked dismissively away over her shoulder, leaving the smile behind, unimportant, forgotten.

At dinner she found that Baba in no way resembled a whippet. He was an enormous black-haired man with huge pendulous cheeks and a moustache drooping down towards an egg-shaped body. As he appeared entirely unconscious of her existence, she was able to examine him with unembarrassed care. He reminded her of somebody. Who? At last, she remembered. Tenniels' walrus. Pleased with her acumen, she was about to tell him of her discovery when she realized he might find it rude. This further narrow escape unnerved her, and surely he must think her rude anyway, sitting there staring at him. She said the first thing which came into her head:

'What are you reading now?'

Baba, loudly sucking his Scotch broth out of his spoon, paid not the slightest attention. Perhaps he was deaf. Waiting till his soup was finished, the room quieter, she asked him, in a louder voice, the same question.

Again, no recognition.

Her good manners outraged, she leant forward and said slowly and distinctly, unfortunately in one of those silences that fall without warning on large companies,

'WHAT ARE YOU READING NOW?'

There was suppressed laughter. Baba, without a change of expression, lifted up his chair and turned its back to her. A moment later, the shooting man on her right nudged her sharply and said in a worried voice:

'I say, you ought not to ask Baba questions like that, he'll think you're trying to make fun of him.'

Then he turned his back as well.

After dinner, all the young people were shepherded into the drawing room where they pulled a large number of chairs into a rough circle. Pencils and sheets of paper were handed round.

'Now,' said cousin Mary in her impatient voice, 'you all play the dictionary game, don't you?'

Her intonation plainly conveyed she would have little patience with those who did not. Ignorant, alarmed and embarrassed, Charlotte sat silent. She tried to pick up the rules of the game. Luckily, it did not seem difficult. An obscure word was read out, whose meaning nobody except herself seemed to know. Triumphantly she wrote it down and when the papers had all been handed in, innocently asked how many points she had won for her knowledge. To her dismay, her question caused everyone to start shouting and cousin Mary to say:

'Oh dear, you are a silly girl. I should have thought your mother's daughter would have been brighter,' and, looking angrily at Charlotte, said to her son, 'Henry, go and help her.'

It seemed to Charlotte, fighting back tears, that he joined her with reluctance. Despite his whispers she could not quite understand the game, and at the end of the first round had the worst score. Knowing if she stayed a moment longer she would burst out crying, she stood up and walked out of the room. Nobody seemed to notice or care. She climbed the stairs resolutely and tried to walk sedately down the passage, but before she reached her room had to break into a run. Somehow she contrived to bolt the door and lay her head on the pillows before the tears began to flow.

In the morning she waited until the maid had gone before leaning forward in bed hugging her knees and looking out at another blue sky. Then she remembered the events of the previous evening and lay back on her pillow pulling the bedclothes over her head. But in a moment she sat up again. What had she to be sad about?

Yesterday seemed a long time ago. At dinner all she had done was to ask Baba a civil question after he had not spoken for half an hour. He, not she, had been rude. She climbed out of bed and, looking out of the deep-set window, saw the sun shining on the wet grass beyond the shadow of the house. This made her feel better still and she sat down in an armchair which was so hard she wondered what they were made of in Scotland, and planned her behaviour to avoid future disasters. She would wash, dress, go down to breakfast, take care to speak to nobody, come back, put on her tweed skirt and new low rubber-soled shoes and go down to be ready whenever the ladies went out to join the guns. At lunch she would say repeatedly how far fewer grouse there were further north; for some extraordinary reason this remark pleased everybody. Then the thought struck her that after last night's storm of tears her face might look haggard, her eyes red-rimmed, necessitating the wearing of her dark glasses, if she had not lost them.

She went and looked in the mirror and saw to her relief no signs of havoc. Her eyes were clear blue and white without a tinge of redness anywhere. Her skin, now light brown where it was not pink, positively glowed. Perhaps crying was good for her, anyway, she had to admit she looked so pretty it was unnecessary to glance at her confidence book. Full of good resolutions, she walked downstairs to find the shooting party had already left, and the dining room was completely empty except for cousin Mary, cool, beautiful, sitting at the head of the table opening letters. She gave her a friendly smile and said 'good morning' which startled Charlotte to reply loudly 'good morning' not at all in the manner she intended. Then, seeing with some dismay that all the other places had been used, she went and sat down next to her frightening hostess, quietly drank her coffee and ate her toast.

Cousin Mary spoke for the second time: 'So charming, Prince Peter, don't you think? Writes such amusing letters,' and tossed a sheet of paper to Charlotte.

It was a brief, type-written note, stating starkly how the writer had enjoyed his shooting and the lack of birds had not detracted from the pleasure of the very long days on the magnificent moors. It stressed the noisy rattling on the sleeper on the return journey to London and the annoyance caused by the hall porter at Claridges failing to send a hired car to the station, the consequent inconvenience and discomfort of the taxi journey to the hotel. It ended by expressing the hope he would have the pleasure of welcoming her at luncheon in Lausanne in the late autumn. Charlotte read it twice, and even looked on the back to see if there was an amusing drawing or limerick. Nothing. She reread the letter slowly and carefully. At home she would have asked what was funny but she realized this would be extremely unwise. She was determined to be both polite and careful, but not to ingratiate herself by telling a lie or pretending to laugh at nothing.

She decided to compromise and said:

'Thank you, it's very well written.'

Cousin Mary, deep in another letter of thanks, merely murmured:

'Oh good, I was sure you would see his charm, how discerning and appreciative you are.'

There were no further alarms and after breakfast she walked around the four fronts of the house, surrounded on all sides by forest. As there seemed nothing else to do, she went upstairs to her bedroom. The door was ajar, and she could hear the noise of the maids moving about. This was embarrassing, for she found herself always saying to them what a lovely morning it was, which was obvious when it was fine but downright silly when it was raining. She tossed her head bravely and walked in to receive a shock which made her left hand fly up instinctively to cover her mouth, while she stood motionless, her right hand still on the door knob. Two maids were busy in her room, the bed had already been stripped and the sheets lay in a ball on the floor. Her suitcase, resting on the small sofa at the end of the bed, was nearly full and at that very moment her sponge bag and shoes were being inserted in its top. Her light coat lay neatly folded on the hard armchair; on it, equally neat, lay her hat.

There could be no mistake; she had been turned out.

The first thought that rushed to her brain was where could she go? It was nine days before she was meeting her mother in Edinburgh and she had very little money left. Then she settled the problem: she would go back to the temperance hotel in Perth. Eating one full meal a day she should just manage. Her mind relieved, she started to blame herself. How stupid not to have realized how much she had annoyed her cousin William with her misinformation at lunch, or how much she had offended Baba with her tactless question at dinner, and certainly she had been idiotic in that awful game, so why should they want her to stay?

Whatever happened now she must leave with dignity, without tears. Trying to speak in a casual tone, she asked the time of her train. They told her the car was leaving for the station in a quarter of an hour. Remaining calm, she made a precise plan. She would wait in an upstairs sitting room for eight minutes, then put on her hat and coat and say goodbye to cousin Mary.

As the minutes passed slowly, the thought would keep creeping in that she had been unkindly treated and done nothing deserving such a cruel punishment. This made her sorry for herself and, worst of all, brought tears into her eyes, the last thing she wanted. At all events, she must appear unembarrassed; polite, as if being turned out without a moment's notice was nothing to worry about. But, oh dear, would that give the impression that she was turned out of houses all the time, which was certainly untrue. No, she should be polite, formal, but rather cold.

Looking at her watch, she saw it was nearly time for the car and, unless she hurried, would be late and consequently appear reluctant to leave. Dashing downstairs, nearly falling over in her haste, she eventually found cousin Mary in her sitting room. She looked up at Charlotte with amazement.

'Goodness, surely you're not going out on the moors wearing a hat and high-heeled shoes?'

'No, I've come to say goodbye.'

'What do you mean, you're staying ten days, aren't you?'

'They have packed my things.'

'Oh, that idiotic housekeeper, so deaf! She must have thought I said Lady Charlotte, not Lady Constance, who has been here far too long already. Oh, you are a tiresome, silly girl not to tell me about this earlier, now she will miss her train.'

And she did, but Charlotte did not mind, relief was flooding through her veins. She was not a total failure, she would not have to retire to the country, she would not have to spend nine days in that horrible hotel in Perth.

Everyone was amused with the story. The red-haired trio were delighted and said how lucky for them she had not gone, and even Baba gave a mixture between a grunt and a chuckle. In other words she was a great success and loved the next nine days and, to her delight before she left, heard cousin Mary admit between her teeth: 'Suchacharminggirl,socleverandamusing.'

The Intercession

He looked at each picture in turn with a swift appraising glance, not without intelligence, sometimes taking in details she had missed, but without feeling or understanding, never lingering, inspecting, rather in the manner of an officer his drawn-up men. So as usual she was left behind and was still in the first room when he, having finished his tour of the gallery, stood behind her. Remarking it was an interesting collection, he looked at his watch:

'Julia my dear, if we are to cover Assisi before lunch we should leave in half an hour. There is no immediate hurry – take your time as I am going to the local bank. I notice the value of the pound has increased by ten lira; I plan to be back here at eleven-forty-three; we should start then.'

When he had gone she wished she understood art, did not find the comments of catalogues and guide books incomprehensible. Once or twice, especially at the beginning of the holiday, she had been stirred without warning to wonder and enlightenment, thinking she comprehended the beauty in the artist's soul. It was confusing and distressing that usually her favourites received no special mention – were merely attributions, or 'the school of'. It must mean she had no taste.

But anyhow, by now Julia had seen enough pictures. Their tour had lasted two weeks – one remained. How tiring it was moving nearly every day, packing, unpacking, although Charles was no trouble and looked after his own scrupulously neat suitcase. But the tedium of waking up with a lost useless feeling, in a series of hotel rooms. She pulled herself up. It was kind of Charles to have thought of their going 'when we are still young enough to take things in'. Certainly the children would not have enjoyed it. But at the same time she could not help wishing that she was not missing so much of the holidays. They went so quickly, and each time the boys had changed, grown a little older, edged a little further away from her, with secrets of their own she understood by looks she was not intended to understand. What a short time ago they had been hers entirely. Would it be sensible to have another baby? But she had given so much to the two boys, she knew that never again could she feel the same happiness. How sad to watch your children growing up, knowing you had to make them independent, form characters which made them slowly discard you. She loved them so much that every day stolen, when they were still partially hers, was a sad waste.

But it *was* kind of Charles to have taken so much trouble, organizing everything so smoothly: with him tickets were never lost; trains or aeroplanes missed. Fate seemed to give in to him, never playing tricks, realizing his mastery as everything went according to plan. How different he was from her; never could she have made an itinerary in which every hour was accounted for, every distance measured, every journey minutely planned.

Charles, of course, was sensible. If you were going to see a country you might as well see as much as possible. But it would have been nice to have taken a little house on the coast – somewhere, it didn't matter where – even though it was only March. She loved the sea, and how pleasant it would have been to take long walks in the pine woods while Charles worked at all those papers in his briefcase.

They could have had a car and driven away for whole days, but Charles had said a firm base would limit them; she supposed he was right.

'My dear, I don't want to break into your thoughts, but it is now eleven-forty-five and although, as you know, I always leave five minutes for unforeseen events, unless we go soon we shall not arrive on schedule by twelve-thirty. You see, I had planned forty minutes for our inspection of the upper and lower churches and five minutes to climb the hill. It is always wise to be punctual otherwise restaurants incline to give tables away, and I have booked one for one-fifteen. Not that a restaurant is likely to be full at this time of year, but nevertheless it is always wise to stick to rules otherwise you can suddenly find yourself surprised. Do you admire the picture you are staring at?'

He gave it a penetrating look, turning over the pages of his catalogue before snapping it shut.

'Yes, I see it is interesting, but not definitely attributed.'

She mumbled something, feeling guilty – she had hardly seen it – and followed him to the car. When they started he stuck a neat plan of the route to Assisi on the windscreen, with every point of interest marked so at every turn in the road he was able to say with satisfaction: 'That is the tower of . . .' 'There is the castle of . . .'; 'that must be . . . in the distance. Difficult to tell exactly how far it is as the crow flies, but eleven kilometres by road.'

Of course it was always interesting information, and showed how thoroughly Charles went into everything, and why he was Chairman of his family company.

But although it was not hot she felt stifled, airless, and when she looked obediently for some landmark, her eyes would not focus beyond a dead fly on the windscreen. It was the same in San Francesco in Assisi: she heard lectures given in French, English, German and Italian, saw lights turned on and off, and raised heads swivelling this way and that, noticing the upper light casting a shadow over raised eye-sockets, suggesting a tour of the blind. But when she tried to look up she could only see blurs of colour without form. She told Charles she felt a little faint and would sit down.

'Well, it is four hours and seventeen minutes since you completed breakfast, and since I noticed that you only ate half a roll, perhaps it is not surprising. But as I still have thirteen more Giottos to examine and it will upset our plans to return here after luncheon, rest a little; then we shall eat.'

But sitting did not help: something was wrong. Julia felt as strange as when once before she had been about to suffer a realistic dream of her childhood agony. She had hoped it would never recur. But, closing her eyes, it all came back, her worst moments – clear as life. Panic seized her and she gripped the woodwork; the vision was so exact that she relived the scene, could see the playing fields; the long sloping upper field with its running track, the middle field surrounded by beech trees, with a road at the far side, then the lower field for junior girls. On both grounds girls were playing lacrosse. She could hear again the sound of their shouting, moving with the game, changing as the girls ran, their cries sometimes rising high, falling, then gathering force again as if they belonged to a variable wind. She could see all the fields distinctly, although she was playing on the bottom ground. Yes, there was the headmistress coming through the garden into the centre field, passing the pavilion, just as before, beckoning to Miss Sprite, the games mistress, who waves the girls to play on. Then Miss Sprite calls out 'Julia', takes her lacrosse stick, and as the game continues, the headmistress holds her hand while they walk away together. But despite Miss Sprite's whistling and encouraging shouts, the game stops and the girls gather in little groups, gossiping. The headmistress and the girl walk up past the pavilion; turn through the garden and into the study lined with books, above which are endless rows of photographs of groups of girls, and over the mantelpiece a bat, inscribed: 'From Denis Compton to Miss Eileen Horlock, one of the straightest bats in England.' Then she looks at the headmistress whose mouth is working in a funny way, as she tells her to be brave and behave as her mother would have wished, for now she is dead.

Charles was walking towards her looking at his watch again. How many times, she wondered, did he look at it every day. He stopped and asked, with obvious disapproval at their not having done so, if no one had objected to her sitting in the stalls; when she did not answer he said coldly that anyhow they ought to be getting along, luncheon was in five minutes, and they still had to climb the hill.

As usual he ordered the food for both of them, and began one of his lectures; but today she made only a token attempt to listen while he told her about St Francis, Giotto, St Claire and Goethe. Sometimes she felt guilty if her mind strayed when he was imparting useful information – he had read the guide books so carefully.

But today the dream had filled her with dread and a sense of foreboding, as the day after the first dream her father had died. She merely automatically inclined her head while he talked.

After carefully adding up and paying the bill, he said: 'I think you still look a little tired, so while I climb to the top of the old tower it would be wise for you to rest, in fifty minutes we start for Spoleto.'

He did not know that she had decided nothing would make her stay with him until the meaning of her dream was settled. She sat down, unconscious of those around her, on stone steps leading up to a house in the piazza, and gave her mind up to the fears she had pushed away. Her dream could only be a warning that someone she loved was to die. It was a moment for honesty so she had no fears for Charles. But her heart turned over when she thought of her sons: was one of them to die? As little children they had been so close; she had to force herself to be interested in anybody else.

An idea came to her. She looked around desperately for somewhere to pray. Perhaps she could die – what a wonderful relief if God would grant that: leaving her sons to look after each other was the best she could hope for. They would give each other support in the same way the three of them had kept their little world inviolate. She looked around for a church. How strange none was in sight; for the last week the whole of central Italy had consisted of churches. She must find one to tell God she was willing to die; so she asked a passer-by, not shy for once of her halting Italian. He looked at her oddly and pointed at a building across the road she had thought was a Roman temple. The question now was to get there. She felt strange and ill and did not want to faint until she was in the church and had prayed for her sons' lives. As she walked across the street the stones seemed to heave and tower, like waves that at any moment would bear down and crush her. She reached the steps, climbed, clutched at a pillar of the portico as sanctuary, steadied herself, and entered. The stranger was right, outside it was a temple, inside a church.

Afterwards, when she tried to recollect what had happened, her memory was vague, shocked by the return of the nightmare that morning. As far as she could remember, after she had looked round, she lit the largest candle she could find, dedicating it to the Virgin and, sinking to her knees, prayed that if her dream was a warning of a death in her family, she should be the one to die.

Some vague movement must have disturbed her for she looked up to see the candle had gone out. Getting up and putting more money in the candle box she took out another, but somehow it broke in her hand. Giving up candles she went and sat in the front pew and prayed as she had never prayed before and, when she had finished, tried to open her mind to receive some sign or gesture of hope. It seemed to her that her prayer was answered by a saintly woman with gentle eyes who conveyed it was a woman's duty to suffer as she had suffered for her own son, and her consolation would be found in prayer and humility.

The message was hopeless and Julia winced in helpless despair before she became conscious of another presence who seemed, as it were, to elbow the Virgin aside and stand before her; a strong, harsh personality whose thoughts she could read:

'Why do you bother to waste your time asking a favour of this poor woman who never did anything but weep, even when her son was tortured to death before her eyes. We both exist by belief; without it we die. I retain a certain power this day as it was my birthday, a day of festival, celebration, offerings and prayers. The intensity of that belief lingers on; pray to me not her. I aided my friends, she wept for hers.'

No words were spoken but the meaning was clear as crystal in Julia's mind. She did not know if she was shocked, mad or dreaming.

Startled by a change of atmosphere she looked up to see in the dusk a glittering, helmeted woman, brave, triumphant, with an owl on her shoulder. Dazzled, she closed her eyes, and decided that, even if the vision was the antic of an overstretched mind, it had a strength and glory that offered hope. She turned from the Virgin and prayed with all her heart to the newcomer.

Gradually she felt more peaceful and believed her wish was granted. The boys wouldn't die – it never occurred to her to think of herself. Getting up she walked calmly out of the church at the moment the sun came out of the clouds, a good omen.

On the way to Spoleto, Charles explained the route on another home-made map. Julia did not even bother to listen. He noticed and asked sharply if she had heard what he had said.

'No,' she said, turning, looking him straight in the eyes. 'No, I was thinking of something else.'

Surprised at this unheard-of reply, he said nothing – merely pursing his lips before pulling the map off the windscreen and putting it in his pocket. After that, he drove in absolute silence with a tight look on his face, occasionally giving her sidelong glances of incomprehension and irritation.

But after a time she turned to him and said:

'Do you know anything about a Roman temple – now a church in Assisi?'

The car gave a little jump forward as he put his foot down in surprise.

'Yes,' he replied in a cold voice, 'if you had been yourself – and I must comment on your unusual mood today – you would have heard me at lunch tell you that during Goethe's visit to Assisi, he visited the church to which you refer, St Maria Sopra Minerva, and afterwards declined to visit St Francesco lest his impression of Assisi should be spoiled. I looked it up this morning in my guide books and classical dictionary; it was built by the Emperor Augustus at about the time of the birth of Jesus Christ. Virgil tells us that Minerva was the goddess of handicrafts and war, and a member of the great triad with Juno and Jupiter. The celebrated day of fiesta, the twenty-first of March, was held by many to be her birthday. It is uncertain if this is correct – today is the twenty-first of March.'

He imparted this information in a flat teacher's voice which made all facts, however interesting, tedious, but he was now in a better mood; there was nothing he liked better than giving information.

He concluded, 'You may check what I have told you in the guide book which is on the seat behind. I believe you will find I am substantially correct, except I had forgotten to say that she was a Roman adoption of Pallas Athene and consequently upon occasion violent. Is there anything else?'

'Oh, no,' she said slowly, 'you have told me all I want to know. I am tired to death.'

When they arrived she went straight to her room and undressed in front of him – something she had never done, but it did not matter now – before climbing naked into bed, although it was only mid-afternoon. Charles, dumbfounded, looked at her with definite disapproval.

'I want to be alone,' she said, 'to be completely by myself. Alone.' Then she fell into a dead sleep.

Having toured the town without the pleasure of an audience, he decided to wait until the next day before calling a doctor. But in the morning it was the hotel manager who woke her in a state of wild excitement, to say that her husband had been killed before breakfast, knocked over by a car as he crossed the road looking the wrong way. How unlike him, she thought.

After she had identified the body, and agreed it should be buried in Italy – there seemed no purpose in bringing him back to England – the police asked if they could do anything.

'Yes,' she said, 'I would like a taxi to go to Assisi.'

Inside the church, she stood for a moment with her back to the door, paused, thought; then bought another large candle and sat down on the same pew. This time she held the candle and thanked Minerva (without even a thought of sacrilege) that her husband and not one of her sons had died. If she had hoped for some response from the candle, some sign or vision or phantom, she was disappointed; the church was empty, dead. But she had given thanks, and could do no more. A weight had been lifted from her mind; she felt happier than she had done for years.

On Julia's return to England she was sympathetically received by her few friends as a sorrowing widow who would be lost without Charles. To their astonishment she replied with perfect frankness, 'Not at all. I never liked Charles. I married him against my own wishes and am relieved he is dead.' She followed this up by saying, as if to stress her relief and pleasure, that she was glad certain formalities had necessitated going to Rome, for she had loved her visit. As for the future, she was now determined to set up a little pottery workshop which had always been her ambition. These startling statements excited considerable interest, and a number of casual friends telephoned to ask her to dinner. She went, confident and definite, a changed woman whose transformation was the subject of many enjoyable discussions and theories to which she gave no further fuel by remaining silent about her experience in the church.

But if her acquaintances were intrigued and pleased, her husband's family were outraged. Immediately on her return to England she visited Charles' lawyer and arranged for a reading of his will. It turned out as he had promised, he had left her everything to avoid death duties. The lawyer then took her into another room and produced a letter to her in Charles' handwriting suggesting the management of his monetary affairs, investments etc. should be left in the hands of his broker, and she should give her bank manager a power of attorney to raise capital for her own needs or for those of his mother and two uncles in case of any unfortunate eventuality.

She asked the lawyer if this letter had any legal authority. He hummed and hawed, put his fingers together, and said 'No.' She tore the paper up, threw the bits in the wastepaper basket, and further flabbergasted him by firmly announcing that when the will was proved she intended to take over the Chairmanship of the company at Slough.

That evening she wrote to her mother-in-law turning down the idea of a memorial service as, due to Charles' unpopularity, the church would be empty, and further stated that her house – now Julia's property – would be put on the market in a year's time. If she needed money to rehouse herself, Julia would be prepared to purchase some of her minority holding in the Slough company.

Her sons found to their astonishment, that a weak, sentimental and faintly cloying mother had changed, without warning or reason, into a practical and ambitious friend, helping them in every possible way and making it plain she was anxious they should take over the running of the company when they had adequately prepared themselves by working in every department.

These events took place some years ago. Her sons have taken over the business in Slough, and she has since married a man ten years younger than herself, an excellent glazier. They work together in what is now a small and successful factory. The marriage is happy, and his only regret is that on her annual mid-March holiday to Italy she insists on leaving him behind. He has no idea why, and is too frightened of her to ask.

1 August 1918

In August 1918 the property of Kolotovka, preserved by its remoteness from even the backwaters of provincial life, lay some four hundred miles to the east of Moscow, and some forty miles from the little town of Saltykov. It was not by Russian standards a large property, supporting before the emancipation of the serfs two hundred souls.

The house, bordered on three sides by a fertile peninsula of three thousand acres, was contained by a river which, after many turns and marriages, emptied itself into a tributary of the Volga. On the far side lay an outcrop of small wooded hills forming a trackless barrier to the west. To the east ran for many miles a dark whispering forest of pines through which meandered the only road out of the settlement, frequently blocked in winter by fallen trees and snow drifts.

The long, low, two-storeyed house, built of white painted boards with a wooden portico facing south, stood on a little hill. At this front, in a small hedged garden, there was a stone pond with a cherub standing on a rock grasping a fish which was forever about to throw up a spout of water. The hope was still-born. The fountain had never been connected to the water supply.

Some fifty yards lower down the hill, again facing the centre of the house, was a large white wooden gate guarding the entrance to and from an old lime avenue clearly intended to enclose a front drive. The road had never been built. The remainder of the garden has been visited many times by readers of Russian novels of the nineteenth century. It stretched around the house on sloping ground, hand-mown by scythes, filled with great clumps of lilac, dogwood and bushes of entangled roses. At three vantage points stood pine-log summer houses covered with honeysuckle. An immense spreading old oak dwarfed clumps of birch and alleys of aspen and limes. Leading from the garden on the western side was an orchard of two acres. The trees were of different ages – the fallen ones had always been immediately replaced. Nowhere was a dead tree or shrub to be seen.

To the east of the shrubberies lay a large pond dug by serfs in the time of Catherine the Great, surrounding a small island which was connected to the land by a bridge two planks wide with a sturdy handrail. At one time it had been adorned by a Chinese pagoda but this, retaining a few tawdry elegances, had long since been converted into a poultry house.

By late summer the island was bare of vegetation, and even in spring it had a messy and muddy look due to the large numbers of ducks, the especial joy of the proprietor's wife, Princess Irena Petrovna Kropotkin. Every morning she walked down through the garden to the pond, carrying in her hand a basket of maize which she would scatter among her surrounding pets. On certain days she would not appear and Grigori, one of the farm men, would take her place and quickly and expertly catch and wring the necks of several fat young ducklings waddling expectantly around his feet. Apart from fears for the health of her numerous dogs, the death of her ducklings and young poultry was the principal sorrow of her life.

The buildings surrounding the great yard at the back of the house were as well-kept as the grounds. The thatch was in perfect condition, the timbers of the great barn covered a dry floor separated by brick partitions on which were laid sacks of the remnants of last year's harvest of maize, wheat, oats and barley. In another side-house were stacked barrels of salted herrings and beef, while from the ceiling hung whitewashed hams. Next to the house was a fruit room where Irena Petrovna would go at the first snows and spend whole mornings individually turning round the apples and pears. Adjoining it was a still room lined with row upon row of bottles of fruit and jam. There appeared no end to the stores and provisions. From the house could be seen, through the trees, swaying fields of ripe corn awaiting the reaper. On every side there was evidence of foresight and good husbandry.

Some two hundred yards down the hill behind the outbuildings lay the village, very different from the broken tumbledown collection of wooden shacks with holes as chimneys which were still so common at that time in Russia west of the Urals. The originator of all this prosperity was Prince Dimitri Ivanovitch Kropotkin, father of the present proprietor, who had died thirty years before. Born in 1810 and sickened by the inefficiency and barbarism of Russian rural life he had, on succeeding to his estates at the age of thirty, visited England. The magnificent-looking young giant, fierce at first sight but with a singularly sweet smile, was a social comet, a matter of transient interest to him. But his practical idealism was fired by the neat villages of the gentry and the writings of John Stuart Mill, Cobbett, Cobden and the English radicals of the early nineteenth century. Moved by the enthusiasm of good intentions he returned to Russia, resigned his Army commission and determined to retire to live on and improve his estate. A portrait of him as a young man shows him with a proud aquiline nose, a rather thin mouth below a black drooping moustache, looking every inch that not uncommon contradiction, an aristocratic autocratic liberal.

Understanding the permanence of his intentions his mother arranged, with his passive agreement, a marriage with a Countess Soloka, an heiress, faithful and timid, one of those women who believe they are born to agree with their chosen husband and mother his children. Alas she was barren, causing her husband such distress that he filled every moment of his days with estate work, ignoring his wife, giving her a feeling of inadequacy and uselessness. Prince Dimitri never hid his disappointment, and eventually his neglect and transparent disdain reduced her to a fluttering nonentity, making annual journeys to distant shrines, constantly praying before new icons and allowing herself to be deceived and robbed by every mendicant charlatan.

The Kropotkins were an old and distinguished family, at one time grand Princes of Smolensk; their power had declined as that of the Romanovs had risen. Prince Dimitri was a descendant of a younger branch. His mother, also an heiress, had given him a substantial sum of money to which he added, without consulting his wife, by immediately selling her country property to enable him to have adequate financial resources to realize his ideals. He brought back from England not only radical beliefs but a large folio containing plans of cottages and small houses for 'workmen of all stations in the service of the nobility and gentry'. Choosing a large flat space at the bottom of the hill he laid out a village green – the only one ever seen in Russia – and built around it a collection of model cottages. Apart from occasionally substituting thatch for slates the cottages were in every sense identical to the plans, and, to the wonder of the peasants, a model English village sprung up in the heart of holy Russia. By the time of his death in 1890 no less than seventy-two houses of various fanciful designs had risen facing the green, each with a front and back garden.

Certainly the greatest excitement of his lifelong devotion to building was when he decided to remember the passing of the Emancipation Act by creating what would now be called an amenity centre, consisting of a small stone school and a white boarded church with a little spire, both dwarfed by the stone church hall which rose beyond and which was exactly copied from one on a Lancashire baronet's estate. It stood facing south with a large Gothic window rising to the height of the vaulted ceiling. An enormous stove was placed at the other end between two bookcases filled with neglected tracts. During the work the peasants believed their late master had adopted the pagan English religion and was building a palace to dwarf the church of his fathers. These rumours were only finally set at rest by the arrival two years later of a full-size billiard table from England, with two men from Manchester to put it together. When their job was finished, although the rules were unknown to them, they were forced to play exhibition rounds of both snooker and billiards in front of the bemused and ungrateful villagers. However, what did take the peasants' fancy were the varnished wooden cues shining to their tapered ends. The coloured balls were equally popular with their children. In a year no cues remained to hit the balls and no balls remained to be hit.

It was suggested the hall should be used for celebrations following village weddings. Overawed by the bleak room the peasants decided its height took the taste and effect out of vodka; this was rejection. From then on it remained empty. The Prince shrugged his shoulders. He had provided a civilized amenity – one day he hoped it would be used.

News travels quickly even in remotest Russia, and his idea of building a billiard room for his peasants caused many a laugh in the houses of the gentlefolk and confirmed their opinion that he was a positive madman, a belief already held by every landowner within a radius of one hundred miles.

After all, he had for years vociferously supported the emancipation of the serfs but, after the hated Act was passed, at the first meeting of the provincial council of nobility in 1862, he declared in anger the terms of emancipation 'are grossly unfair to the peasants who will be infinitely worse off than before, and if they uncomprehendingly accept the dishonest scheme for gratuitous holdings which I know in places will be forced on them, they will unwittingly place themselves in a position as binding and as shameful as their earlier status. The long and short of the Act will be to reduce, not increase, land farmed by the peasants.'

He continued that it was his intention to give each of his peasants a larger holding out of his own land, that he would not ask for redemption money, and that by the reclamation of forest and bog he hoped to increase the size of their holdings still further.

'The alternative is to create a starving land-starved peasantry ripe for revolution, full of hatred, on whom you will *always depend* although you cannot understand that simple fact.'

There was silence as he walked upright out of the hall. When it was certain he was out of hearing there was a regular hubbub. Speech after speech was made attacking his theories. His fellow landlords were furious. Once the Emancipation Act was law it was the end of paternalism as far as they were concerned. The peasants had been freed to look after themselves and live on what the Tsar had been stupid enough to give them. As the years passed his prophecies proved accurate; many landlords spent their redemption money and found they had to rely – to work their land – on free rebellious men, not frightened serfs. Their farms suffered, their incomes declined and many of them were ruined. This last class vitriolically insisted on the sly madness of Prince Dimitri, forgetting the profitability of his farms, the most efficient in the province.

One afternoon in summer when the Prince was in his sixty-sixth year, he was down by the river supervising the draining of an area of marshland. He walked with a slight stoop now, although when erect he still stood over six foot two. It was a hot day, the mosquitoes and flies were maddening, and standing bareheaded in great leather boots he frequently passed his mud-encrusted hands over his head and across his moustache to wipe away the moisture, caring little about the dirt smeared over his white hair and face.

All at once the peasants stopped work and stared, with the intense interest of the countryman, at a horse and rider galloping towards them. A house servant jumped off and hurriedly whispered a few words in the Prince's ear. He immediately mounted and cantered, in less haste, away. The man, pleased at the interest excited, related in hushed tones his news to the curious workmen.

The Princess had fallen over in the garden and was unconscious. By the time her husband arrived back she was lying in one of the downstairs bedrooms. Pushing aside the chattering maids carrying towels and icepacks and getting in each other's way, he looked down in a detached way on the withered, twisted and contorted face, the pinched cheeks, the thin neck, feeling no emotion of pity or sorrow. The doctor arrived, examined her, pulled down the sides of his mouth and stated the obvious. She had suffered a severe stroke and was unlikely to recover.

Prince Dimitri was deep in thought for the next two days. He ate absent-mindedly, drank no spirits, continued with his draining operations, but with a distracted and thoughtful rather than sorrowful air. On the third morning he was woken by a clamour of female voices and shrieks and sobs coming from her bedroom. Putting on a dressing-gown he walked downstairs and saw the female house servants simulating with loud cries the grief he doubted they felt. It seemed ridiculous to lament insincerely and he silenced them with a scowl before placing his hand on her forehead, but quickly drew back, momentarily shocked by the coldness of her brow. It had given him a physical shock to feel dead flesh. Then a dramatic event occurred, causing endless discussion in the village for years to come. All the watchers agreed, as he looked down on his wife a slow smile came over his face as if he was thanking her for solving a problem, long a source of trouble and pain. He ate a good lunch and continued with the draining in the afternoon.

That night he sat down and wrote a letter to Bavaria addressed to a woman who, forty-five years ago, had married a Galitzine and was for the next ten years, until her husband's death, one of the toasts of Moscow and Petrograd. She was beautiful as only Bavarians can be – tall, slim, with ash-blonde hair, black eyebrows and a pale golden skin which retained its colour even at the end of a Russian winter. Quick-witted, elegant, and with the gaiety of her mother, a celebrated beauty at the French Court, her charm was irresistible. At the age of twenty he had fallen passionately in love with her.

Although they were of the same age she appeared older and wiser, and uncritically and sympathetically understanding the problems of his young life. When he realized that she would never be his mistress she became instead the confidante of his love affairs, 'my consolations' as he called them. She endlessly tried to tone down his dangerous idealism:

'What good can you do in Siberia? What good can you do in prison?' Their friendship lasted for the period of her stay in Russia. She felt protective towards the fervent straightforward young man, half-European in his outlook, kind in his rough way, and unusually sympathetic to the peasants whom she hated to see treated little better than dogs.

Then her husband died and despite, it was said, the Tsar ordering her to stay and bring up her children as Russians, she returned to Bavaria at about the time Prince Dimitri's own father died. (Her departure was one of the reasons for his year-long visit to England.) When he returned to Russia it felt as if a dagger had been driven into his heart when he heard she was to marry a Bavarian, and he did not object when his mother arranged a marriage to a pretty, pale suitable girl. He never forgot his first love despite his frenetic devotion to manual work, and now turned to her as he had forty years before.

My dear Elizabeth –

If I may so call you after your second marriage. Let me tell you why I write. I married a woman whom God chose to make barren. I was never unkind to her but could not forgive her a fault for which she was not responsible. I always passionately desired a son and, although now sixty-five, have no reason to believe I cannot father one. I have never forgotten the friend of my youth or the love I felt for you. How different it might have been if you had loved me. I have lived long enough in Russia to know the hopelessness of the Russian character and desire to mitigate it by marrying a Bavarian of noble birth inspired, I may say, by my memory of you. I am aware that at sixty-five I cannot hope, indeed do not wish to marry a beautiful young girl. What I desire is a wife in her mid-thirties without the ties of children who will be content to have mine. I will die happy if I have a son. Can you think of a well-born woman who could fulfil my needs? I plan as soon as the funeral is over – I am too old to waste time hanging about – to travel to Bavaria, hopefully to visit you. Could you leave an answer at the German Embassy in Petrograd where I will be next week, settling the affairs of my late wife?

Any wife of mine will have to understand I am now a dedicated countryman and cannot face a social life in Moscow. I would also be grateful if you could think of a suitable land agent to bring back with her. As it is unlikely I will live more than fifteen years it will comfort and reassure her when I am dead to have a fellow countryman running her affairs.

I conclude by saying that I regret I cannot send my compliments to your husband. I successfully put his name out of my mind when I heard of your marriage and I do not know if he is alive or dead.

I am, yours respectfully, Dimitri Ivanovitch Kropotkin.

The morning after his arrival in Petrograd he hastened, as soon as he had finished breakfast, to the German Embassy but as he neared the gate saw to his dismay that it was only half past eight, and was forced to drive up and down for another hour before he thought it proper to go in. A letter awaited him. He thrust it into his pocket, gripping it until he was back in the hotel room. Then, trembling, he sat down on an armchair and read and reread the letter, written in French, whose elegant style is inadequately reproduced in this mundane translation.

My dear Dimitri –

I read your letter with difficulty as I have not spoken Russian for years. How can you flatter yourself I could forget one who was, and I can read still is, straightforward to the point of rudeness, and who, without forethought or tact, always said what he thought? But think how, if I had married you, my poor dead ghost would have wept in her grave to see you rushing off to find a new wife the day after my death! I admit I have often thought of you, indeed you are one of the few fond recollections I have of my married life in Russia. I trusted your affection and felt for you perhaps more deeply than I ever showed. How long ago it was and how disappointed you will be when you see the old hag into which I have turned. But if you wish to come to Bavaria I insist you come to our house in the country which is only twenty miles from Munich. The address you will see at the top of this page.

In a strange way your letter is the answer to my prayers; I am deeply concerned about the future of a dear cousin of my husband's, Sophia D'Ortenbourg, thirty-seven years old, whose husband died last year. Poor thing, she always pined for the country and children but was forced to live a never-ending social life while her husband spent their fortunes on frivolities and excesses which had little to do with her happiness. To put it delicately he was a friend of King L –– and shared his tastes so you will comprehend why she had no children! At any rate he is dead, she is almost destitute and, as is always the case when circumstances change for us poor women, neglected unkindly. I cannot pretend her heart was never elsewhere engaged. It was, for a time, to a man whom I considered undeserving of her affection – and alas, my doubts were proved correct by his behaviour when her husband died. You see I have been completely frank with you. It is as well you should hear from me what others will delight to spitefully hiss in your ear. Whether she will accept your offer, of course, is another matter and depends on whether you have changed as much as I have. If so she will certainly not accept. But if you remain as insistent and compelling as I remember, you should be able to persuade her to exchange her present dependency on the charity of others for the charming, if rural, home I remember you loved so much. Of one thing you can be sure, she will want no more frivolities. She is fair-haired, well-formed and handsome – you will be a fortunate man if you can win her affections.

Ah, how I hated your country. One by one the Grand Dukes attacked me. And I was even informed that the head of the family would honour me with his affection, which he did – even going so far as to try and prevent my leaving! I don't think I ever told you of these things, fearful that public knowledge of my disdain might cause the family to wreak vengeance on my husband who, in retrospect, was deserving of anything they might have done to him!

We shall be here until the end of September and my husband joins me in hoping you will arrive whenever you please. He also asks me to inform you he is alive and well, his name is Max Ernst and he looks forward to welcoming you, one of the few Barbarians I have ever spoken of with affection. As for myself I look forward with eagerness to the renewal of a friendship which always gave me pleasure, only mitigated by the fear that my appearance may frighten you out of the house.

I am, your old and trusted friend, Elizabeth, and my last name is – so you will not in your tactless way ask my husband –Waldbott de Bassenheim.

P.S. I find in my typically selfish way I have dwelt on myself without a thought of the steward I have in mind. Again your request is opportune. We have here the son of the head agent. Three years ago, at the age of twenty-two, he was engaged to a local beauty with hair the colour of mine when I was young, worn in long plaits down her back. Then the poor boy was kicked by a horse and emasculated (how I do seem to dwell on indecorous matters). As a result he had no alternative but to break off the marriage and has now grown fat, his voice shrill. He continues to work hard and do everything asked of him, but he has a puzzled, hurt look in his blue eyes and I think would love to be a thousand miles from here; so you may find your success in this direction will be easier gained.

Dimitri looked at his watch, the date on the top of his newspaper, and promptly wrote to thank her and her husband for their kind invitation, and to say that unless the unexpected occurred he would arrive for luncheon on the sixteenth of August. The memory of his wife faded from his mind, and he set off for Munich believing that his life would begin again.

As he drove out on the morning of the sixteenth he kept telling himself that it was not his old love he was going to see and marry, but possibly a disappointing alternative. The meeting of the old friends was an anti-climax, as such occasions usually are. Despite the passing of thirty-five years he had still thought of Elizabeth as a fair-haired beauty wearing an emerald tiara. When they met he saw a distinguished-looking woman in a dark dress buttoned up to the neck. Her hair was grey but the dark eyebrows and blue eyes were unchanged. She was far fatter than he had expected. She saw the same giant, bent now, with white hair, a white moustache and deep lines scarring his face. They were soon on good terms although the magic had faded. This awareness of disappointment made them both try harder to show affection and he soon noticed, for reasons she would not divulge, her anxiety that Sophia should return to Russia as his wife.

After lunch he interviewed the agent, who seemed as sensible and practical as Elizabeth had written, though she had omitted to mention his magnificent thick mane of fair hair, which gave him a leonine look. He agreed at once to come to Russia. It was a good omen.

His intended bride Sophia was much as he had hoped, fair-haired and blue-eyed, with arms and legs a little too thick for beauty but showing the strength he thought necessary in a woman whose function it was to bear his son. He had brought with him water colours of his house, the farm, the drawing room, his late wife's sitting room with the section of her sitting in a chair carelessly washed out. She decided to marry, not because she loved him or thought she ever would – for his determination and self-obsession frightened her – but because she was thirty-seven, wished to have children and could think of no suitable man in Bavaria or Germany who would marry her. The decisive factor was that her friend of ten years now loved a young girl. She could see no other way to forget him, to avoid the humiliation of seeing him in hated company.

Elizabeth persuaded them to get married in the chapel of the castle, a private ceremony attended only by Sophia's family, Elizabeth and her husband. Dimitri planned immediately to return to Kolotovka. Elizabeth was firm:

'Sophia has always wished to go to Venice. Once you get her into Russia you will never let her out again – this is her last chance. I tell you if you are going to have a happy marriage you must make certain concessions and the first one, which I insist on, is your taking her to Venice for a week.'

It was hot and the canals smelt, but Dimitri to his surprise enjoyed the romance of the city, the long lazy gondola trips to the Lido and Torcello, the Byzantine glory of St Marks which made him smell Russia. Sophia revived old fires within him. Perhaps no women in Europe make better wives than Bavarians and he tasted, for the first time in years, the pleasure of making love to a civilized woman. And so to please her he stayed on another week although he was beginning to worry about the harvest.

Afterwards they returned to Munich to stay one night with Elizabeth in her town house and collect Hans Dietrich, the new agent, at the station. His appearance had changed. The thick thatch of blond hair had vanished at the hairdresser's. His head was shaven. Sophia was shocked; his beauty had gone with his hair. She did not know that the shaving of his head was a symbolic gesture of dedication to work. He had purposely destroyed his good looks to end the enquiring glances from girls to which he could give no answer.

The harvest was in when they arrived and Sophia threw herself enthusiastically into country life. She saw with delight the internal mismanagement of the household, the scarcity of home-made jams and bottled fruits, the mis-hanging of the hams in the wrong temperature. She loved the garden, the countryside, the walks in the woods where the gentle singing of the pine trees reminded her of the beloved mountains of Bavaria. Dimitri was busy all day in the fields, as the period of autumn ploughing, harrowing and sowing was a race against the early snowfalls. It pleased Sophia that he worked alongside the peasants, unconscious of any social superiority, claiming no privilege of birth. At the same time she was relieved that his authority was accepted without question, and that he was treated with shades of deference and affection. She had only one fear; the headman whom Dietrich was to replace had not retired and Sophia was pleased to see that her husband sheltered her fellow countryman from the antagonism natural in an isolated community.

Dietrich worked swiftly and efficiently and appeared to learn Russian quickly, dividing his time every evening between Russian grammar and carpentry, ensuring himself no time to think. Then in the last week in October the first snows came. Sophia was used to cold weather in the mountains at home but in Russia it overwhelms, destroying in its pitiless onslaught all joy. But she was determined not to be defeated. A large trunk of desirable books had been brought from Munich. She had left until the cold weather the redecoration of the drawing room and the carefully planned reconstruction of the kitchens, sculleries and storeroom. All this, she hoped, would see her through the long months which lay ahead. To her surprise Dimitri was not as difficult to live with as she had feared and in December she triumphantly told him she was pregnant. It never entered his head that he might not have a son and she now had the additional task of preparing her baby's clothes and starting a correspondence with Elizabeth concerning a suitable German nanny to come and look after the baby.

But even with all these distractions the winter was long and tedious and she found herself at times suffering from homesickness and the gloom which permeates the land-locked in Russia.

All of a sudden spring came and an awakening garden. She immediately started work. The orchard was selectively felled and replanted, the pond and cupid cleaned and the ridiculous old Chinese folly turned into a house for water fowl. She also persuaded Dimitri to build a school and a house for the teacher. (The peasants were mistrustful and for years few children attended.)

The German nurse arrived in August, and the baby was born two weeks later, a son christened Pavel Dimitrich Kropotkin. In the next year she had a daughter and, in subsequent years, two more. The house was full of noise and screams but Dimitri did not mind. He would often stand silent, looking down on his son. The German nanny said with a worried look that he was the best baby she had ever known – in her career all other children had cried cutting their teeth. The father decided that the child's silence suggested courage, a good sign.

After the great event life went on as before. Sophia threw herself into the village life, household works, long talks with the nanny, and very soon preparations for her second pregnancy. Despite these interests she sometimes longed for the life she had previously hated, and once she hopefully suggested they should pay a visit to Elizabeth.

Her husband shook his head, not wishing to see his shattered dream again. She realized she was an exile but she had a son, was having another baby and respected her husband. Things could have been a lot worse. She must make the best of it.

Prince Dimitri taught Dietrich everything he knew, delighted by the intelligence of his pupil. The men soon came to respect him – it was against their nature to like a German but he was soon accepted. Perhaps it was his natural goodness and fairness and the amazing fact that he never tried to take advantage of them or the Prince but rather increased their profits by good management and procuring the finest seed and new machinery. In the eyes of the women his voice and injury gave him the status of a man of God, and he gave to every one of them in the village a hand-made little box, made by himself, on their namedays.

After five years of marriage and four children Sophia made another suggestion to her husband; it would be advantageous to make the estate self-sufficient. Already it had a school, a store, a carpenter, two builders, a blacksmith – why not a small hospital? She could not help noting how often, and for no particular reason, children seemed to suffer dietary ailments, how the peasants' little scratches often became septic and, worst of all, how frequently young children died, events tragic to her but hardly noticed by the careless mothers.

The next year a square one-storeyed hospital was built and an elderly German doctor imported, thereby adding to Sophia's little colony of homelanders. At first the peasants totally ignored the doctor, but Sophia's gentle persuasions and insistence on taking him herself to see sick children and old men showed that cures were possible. After a few years there was hardly a man in the village who would not go to the hospital at least once a year, even if there was nothing wrong with him. With her school, hospital and four children she was now happier than she had ever been and her husband, now over seventy, began to feel at peace for the first time in his life.

In the tenth winter of their marriage Sophia took her three little girls for a drive in her pony cart. It was late in the year, the beginning of October, but mushrooms could still be found in the oldest parts of the wood where the hardwoods grew, reached by a little road on which her pony could not flounder. On the way, without the least warning – it was a calm day – half a fir tree overhanging the road split off and fell on the cart. The mother and three children died instantly.

It was said when her husband arrived his face was as white as his hair. Single-handed, without apparent effort, he moved the huge branch off his family. Seeing there was no hope he walked home without a word, climbed immediately upstairs to the nursery where Pavel was doing his lessons and stood silently weeping looking down on the pale, frightened little boy. He was crying at the thought that his son might have been killed. But he had loved Sophia in his own way and had treated his little girls like pretty dolls to be petted and caressed.

There was no smile on his face this time as he stood looking down on the poor crushed figure of his wife as she lay in her coffin. He looked a sad old man and now, aged seventy-five, had little to live for except his son. He stayed more and more in the house and garden. Twice a week Dietrich would come for two or three hours to describe every detail of the estate work to the Prince, who frequently made suggestions. Even if Dietrich disagreed he did not argue and the orders were scrupulously carried out. His doubts were seldom proved wrong. This he never mentioned but admitted to himself that the Prince's judgement was not what it had been.

Three years later, at the end of October, the old Prince felt a sharp pain in his back. He said nothing but the next week made one of his rare visits to Moscow to see a French doctor, a worker of miracles. He was examined, asked for the truth and was told nothing could be done. He should put his affairs in order. In all probability he would be dead within six months.

All the way back to Kolotovka he thought incessantly of his son. The boy had changed after the death of his mother, retiring into himself, seldom going into the forest or down to the river with the village boys. He had loved his mother and sisters; their death had killed something in him which his father had not been able to revive. The Prince knew that he would never have the son he had hoped for. Pavel's face was a weak caricature of his own, the nose smaller, the mouth looser, the chin weaker. And his limbs were long and puny. Perhaps he had been wrong to marry a second time and father an old man's child. But in his old age he loved him for his gentleness and because he was his only son. Who was to look after him? His first action when he arrived home was to tell Dietrich the truth and send him to fetch a poor relation, a retired captain who lived near Saltykov, a thick-set slow man whose face was so covered in hair you could scarcely pick out a feature. He was a decent, respectable man with a gentle, kindly domestic wife Anna, so anonymous-looking that the more you examined her the less you knew what she looked like. On their arrival Pavel seemed mildly pleased at her fulsome attentions.

The ceaseless pain in the Prince's back increased daily. He arranged for the families in the village to come and pay their last respects. News of his approaching death spread and from distances of up to forty miles peasants walked or drove to say goodbye. Hospitality was offered to all – to the men vodka, to the women tea, to the children cakes. Every visitor, although at first the Prince tried to check them, ended by throwing themselves down to kiss his feet. These moving farewells he found almost unbearable. There was, he thought, one compensation. So unendurable was the pain in his back he only had to allow himself to admit it to dry up the tears which would otherwise have run down his cheeks. As it was he sat upright, thanked every man who had worked for him, and every visitor for their courtesy.

The farewells lasted for three weeks. He had become a living skeleton; his face had fallen in, his nose looked enormous. He noted with sadness that his son shrank back when he went to say goodnight. Sleep was impossible and the dying man knew that time was short. He sent for Dietrich and asked him if it was his intention to return to Germany.

'I ask you this question because my son, at thirteen, has not the vigour I expected.'

Dietrich assured him his life was inexorably bound up in Kolotovka. He promised he would stay with Pavel until death. The Prince thanked him, told him he was to be sole guardian of his son, and to continue to send abroad every year to London a proportion of the profits of the farms. With an effort he slowly stood up and shook the Bavarian's hand. No word was spoken but Dietrich was embarrassed. He realized then that the Prince thought him a better man than he was.

That evening the father went to see his son, gave him his gold watch and advised him stiffly that life was never easy, but to always remember he had the good fortune to be a Kropotkin, a family who had always looked after their dependants. When he was a man he should remember that although the peasants had independence they remained children and he must, by example, ensure their good behaviour and prosperity.

'I have little hope in the future. Years ago I saw the selfishness of our class in freeing the peasants but cheating them out of their land. The tragic effects are to be seen everywhere but here. Never forget it is the Russian landlord who is to blame for the present unrest – do your duty.'

He wished to kiss his son goodbye but knowing it would revolt him, stood back and held out his hand. Pavel, looking down, gave him a limp handshake.

The next morning he was dead. He had gone after dinner to sit in the summer house which looked west over the valley towards the wooded hills beyond the river. He could not have seen his favourite view in the dark but it was said there was a happy look on his cold face.

On the evening that Dietrich was told he was to be the sole guardian of the boy he walked back to his house full of sorrow and pride. He had always tried to hide the mortal blow his emasculation had given his secret hopes. His ambitions had been simple; a happy marriage, a life of hard work and a return to his family fireside at night. When he fell in love with the long-haired beauty, it seemed as if those wishes were about to be realized. The horse kicked him and after the agony was over there was nothing left to hope for.

In the months that followed he felt the despair of a deserted lover and thought of killing himself. The pastor told him that God intended him to suffer and that he was fulfilling his destiny. The consolation was slight. The Prince's offer came without warning. He accepted and threw himself heart and soul into the work of the property and the learning of Russian. He was hard-working, thorough and practical. When he became overseer he would walk over the whole forest and surrounding scrubland, carefully noting what should be retained for woodland, what cleared and drained. Then he carried out an intensive survey of the marshland where frequently he sunk almost out of his depth. Within a year he had worked out a twenty-year programme which provided not only for an increased allocation of land for the peasants, but also of land for the succeeding generation.

During the thirteen years they worked together he never received an angry word from his employer but many expressions of gratitude. They made an ideal partnership. Prince Dimitri was too hot-headed and impulsive to think and plan but had been, until recently, a tiger for practical work. Dietrich had been infinitely touched by the Prince's thanks, but what delighted him above all was his guardianship of young Pavel. The boy's silence and lack of interest was surely a reaction to his father's overpowering personality and to his own poor education. No attempt, in Dietrich's view, had been made by his tutors to interest Pavel in facts and figures, in the classification of data or in the intricacies of modern management. To his great joy the agent imagined a companion whose character he would develop, a replacement for the child he could never have.

As for the retired captain, Vasily Mikhailovich Paklin, Dietrich never understood why the Prince moved him into the house. His wife Anna was a kind woman but hopelessly Russian. Overwhelmed by life, they lived from day to day without purpose or ambition. He would have to be careful the boy did not catch their lassitude.

His fears were justified. Pavel, crushed by the death of his beloved mother and little sisters and terrified even by the memory of his father, came unconsciously under their influence. Their dullness suited him. He found in their company a peace and security he had never known since the terrible day on which he often wished he had died with his mother.

As for the captain, he was pleased at the way things had worked out. His whole life had been a trial. Without a fortune or influential connections, as a young man he was forced into a military career for which he was unsuited. A dreamer, he could happily have lost himself in one of the Government departments. As it was he had to suffer the dreary discipline of army life and at one memorable period, to his dismay, was posted for two years on active service in the Caucasus, an agonizing experience for a natural coward who hated bloodshed. He saw no romance in the wild mountain peaks, the wooden forts, the struggle reminiscent of the Middle Ages. He saw nothing noble in the daring and bravery of the hill tribesmen; the wild beauty of their daughters repelled him. It was with a sigh of relief that he returned to the mundane life of a garrison in central Russia.

Life in the little town was enlivened by the presence of the military and 'the Captain' found himself in demand as a dancing partner and a gentleman to make up numbers at whist and picnics. He was never rude, never argued with his superiors. His colonel, disliking activity, appointed him adjutant. By one of those strange freaks so common in Russian bureaucracy the garrison became forgotten. Some clerk must have lost a relevant sheet of paper. At any rate the colonel remained in his position years after retiring age. Two majors died and were replaced. Far from the sound of gunshot the captain reconstructed himself as a battle-scarred hero. How long the lapse of official memory might have lasted is impossible to tell. But the colonel suddenly died causing a flutter of enquiries – a visitation from a general, the decision to hush up the whole matter, the retirement of the captain who, fifty-five years old and married to the daughter of a small landowner with a little boy of eight, found himself unemployed, homeless, with only a small pension to live on.

That was seven years ago. He had written to the Prince asking if he could give him a home suitable to his miserable income. He received a reply offering a small house near Saltykov. He moved in and for the next six years took a long walk regularly three times a week and regularly three times a week sat all day in the club. On Sunday he attended church. Then his son died. The captain was sad. He was a nice little boy and it upset him to see his wife crying, crying day and night. There was nothing for it but to cut out his walks and go every day for longer periods to the club. He felt too old to father another child and, in any case, did not like a noisy house. As for poor Anna, she was desolate. She looked after the house, she embroidered, but often she just sat weeping, her work on her knees, remembering every moment of her son's fourteen years.

Then came the offer to move to Kolotovka. Anna was delighted at the idea of young Pavel filling her empty life. He accepted her kindnesses with civility and politeness. Sometimes she would read to him; he would listen and thank her. She taught him draughts – he never seemed to mind if he won or lost. She found it difficult to love him. He was so different from her lively, noisy son.

After the death of the Prince the captain left the worldly education of the boy to Dietrich who would come every afternoon when the tutor had finished and take the boy into the forest, to the virgin lands to the north where beeches and oaks and a few giant chestnuts grew. Or he would explain to him the life-cycle of trees and show him men working, asking him to note the rapidity with which their flying axes could fell an eighty-year-old fir tree. After the tree had fallen with a crash he would make him count the rings at the base to tell the exact age, pointing out when the rings were wide it recorded a wet summer, narrow a drought. On other days he would take him down to the fields, going through them one by one with a little instrument in his pocket with which he would delve into the earth, extracting small samples of soil, pointing out their constituents, illustrating the difference from the land lying only a hundred yards away. In summer they would watch the dredging and he would explain why the dykes must be kept open, how soon they blocked, how much the reclamation added to the prosperity of the village and his own land.

A month after his father's death Dietrich took Pavel round all the seventy-two houses in the village – many now belonging to the villagers – introducing him to the peasants by name, showing him on the map exactly where their holdings stood, their size, the additional land he planned to reclaim for them. They stood gaping at the young Prince who listened in silence. Every day ended with an exhausted young man who had been bored to death gently shaking hands with a satisfied Dietrich and politely thanking him.

In the winter of course it was better. So much time had to be spent indoors and he could sit more often by the sofa and quietly read or daydream, with a book open on his knees. But there was still so much to be shown; barns had to be repaired, the methods of avoiding drifts on the roads explained, the horses to be visited in their stables where he would hear talk of the correct quantity of hay to be allocated to various mares and yearlings and stallions, to be followed by endless dissertations on winter feed for the cows! There seemed no end to the facts pushed into his mind. But they never stayed there. He could not remember the quantity of hay it was necessary to make each year or that willows had to be planted along the water courses or that lime trees, not oaks, provided the bees with flowers for their honey in summer. He liked rather to sit with the captain staring at the fire, occasionally hearing an imaginary reminiscence of the terrors of Georgia. He liked to reflect, not to be told dreary facts. But he was mild, good-mannered and tried never to let Dietrich see his dread of the endless educational excursions and his preference for the sofa and fireside.

The captain was content. A year or so after the old Prince's death he put his slippers on and never left the house except on fine days, to sit in a summer house and enjoy his pipe in the evening light. The young Prince would join him, the two sitting in silence. Dietrich had been right. The boy was becoming indolent, showing no sign of his father's enthusiasm. But in his secret heart he subconsciously rejoiced. The property would be under his undisputed control for the rest of his life. He pushed his pleasure indignantly out of his mind.

The captain's lassitude lasted for seven years. Each year he rose a little later, drank his first glass of vodka a little earlier, his last considerably later. One morning his wife found his pillow yellow. Jaundice was diagnosed and in six months he was dead. Anna was asked to stay on. Prince Pavel was twenty and had never grown a beard. If he felt sorrow at the death of his companion he did not show it. Dietrich considered the problem. He would have to take a more active line; Kolotovka should have a mistress. He started going into Saltykov once or twice a week. His fame as a skilful farm manager who would give free advice made him popular. Gradually he became of use to neighbouring landowners. In one of their households he saw a suitable girl, Irena Petrovna Sviyazhshy, who was too shy to speak but had a kind, round face and a friendly smile. Her father was a member of an impoverished but ancient family, claiming descent from Rurik. Dietrich knew the Prince would have considered her a suitable wife for his son. They were married in 1898. In 1900 she went to see her mother and haltingly confessed that her marriage remained unconsummated. She was given an old icon, told to pray before it every night and put her trust in God. The marriage remained unconsummated.

She turned to animals for consolation. Sometimes the way her pets produced offspring with such effortless ease made her burst into tears. She extended her interests to poultry and kept twenty or thirty different types of duck on the pond. It was not enough. Dietrich suggested that she add a room to the school and start a kindergarten class for young children. It was a success and for eighteen years she never missed a day through illness. She adored the little children until they moved to the senior school when she quite lost interest in them, and within a year would hardly recognize those who had been her favourites. The work consoled her for her own lack of children and she grew to pity and love her melancholy husband who would sometimes sit down, stroke her hands and gently smile. They never exchanged confidences.

In 1905 Dietrich asked for a special interview. He spoke of the murder in the previous year of the Grand Duke Serge and the recent bloody, unsuccessful peasants' revolt.

'The old Prince was right years ago,' he told them in the respectful voice he put on when he discussed his late master's opinions, 'the peasants are undernourished, underfed and have not got enough land. The laws of 1893 made things worse. The existing system is not working. Now next year there is to be a redistribution of land. Community holdings are to be ended but the individual holdings will not be economic, nor has the Tsar realized the danger of destroying community holdings. It is a fatal mistake. Belief in the old system lies at the heart of the peasants' philosophy. If the present policy is carried out poverty will increase and I fear a succession of peasant revolutions. One day it will be necessary for you to leave. You can go when you wish – you have a substantial fortune in London.'

Meanwhile he advocated a reduction in the size of the Prince's estate and an increase in the size of individual holdings. He said he wanted them to be aware of the situation. Prince Pavel told him to do what he thought was right and gave up a considerable proportion of his land.

Dietrich made other moves to try and gain the peasants' respect and built from a plan in the old Prince's folio of designs a comfortable copy of a small, early English public house. It was so smart, with brass fittings, that the peasants felt uneasy inside. He was more successful in earning gratitude by his deliberate policy of paying substitutes to serve in the Army instead of the young men from Kolotovka.

Although there was perhaps no landlord in all Russia who did as much for his peasants as Dietrich in the name of Prince Pavel, neither the Prince or his wife became popular. They lacked the common touch of his father, and on their annual visit with Dietrich around the village to discuss household problems they sat close together like frightened children, not knowing what to say. This fear made the peasants despise them and think Dietrich mad not to cheat such innocent simpletons.

The violence increased. Landlords were murdered and upon occasion impaled. Stolypin was shot in 1911 and the secret police frustrated numerous attempts to murder the Tsar and members of the Imperial family. Dietrich simply could not see how, in the absence of radical reform, revolution could be avoided. But the

Tsar and Tsarina resisted all change.

He made contact with a number of businessmen in Saltykov who had formed an anti-revolutionary society. It was not difficult to infiltrate the revolutionary bodies which existed even in the little town and he found, to his surprise, that no less than five of the peasants from Kolotovka were members of societies dedicated to revolution and the overthrow of the Tsar. He noted their names, said nothing and in no way treated them differently.

Duma succeeded Duma without changing the Imperial position. In 1912 there was a famine and many districts suffered starvation. Violence increased and the swords of the Tsar's cossacks were red with blood. But in 1914 the outbreak of war with Germany occasioned a wave of patriotism, regaining the Imperial family some of its lost popularity. Initial success was followed by failures and soon stories came back of the lack of arms, of a shortage of ammunition and the slaughter by Germans of unarmed defenceless soldiers. Rumours swept the country of the treachery of the Empress Alexandra, a German, intertwined with wild tales of Rasputin and his salacious influence. Dietrich could no longer save young men from the Army and was spat upon by the bereaved parents of a young soldier. It made him sad; he had done all he could for Russia for nearly fifty years and this was his reward. He was seventy-four and fat, and so bald he no longer had to shave his head. What could he do if he retired? Where could he go? Anyway, he had promised to stay and he would never break his word.

Dietrich admitted to himself that the young couple – not so young now – were useless, though he loyally did what he could so that the peasants at Kolotovka remained prosperous, while beyond the forest he could see the world falling to pieces. He shrugged his shoulders and sat down at his carpenter's bench and carved beautiful boxes, but for whom? He felt old and tired. The despair passed, but he remained cautious and only visited Saltykov at night to see his business friends. When he heard that the Tsar had taken over the supreme command from the Grand Duke Nicholas he banged his fist on the table: 'Is the man mad to take sole responsibility for the inevitable defeat?'

In March the Tsar abdicated. The Grand Duke Michael refused the throne, Prince Lvov and Kerensky tried inefficiently to rule. The Bolsheviks worked unceasingly. On the sixteenth of April Lenin arrived in St Petersburg in a sealed train, by courtesy of the Kaiser. In May the local papers reported the extraordinary fact that the exile Pyotr Kropotkin, a distant cousin of Prince Pavel's, had returned to Moscow to be met at the Finland station of St Petersburg by a crowd of sixty thousand, headed by Kerensky. The Prince had never heard of him. Dietrich, who had thought him an exiled, powerless idealist, now visualized him as a useful ally.

Throughout the summer the peasants repaid old debts with death. The Tsar and his family were under house arrest. Internally, as rebellious soldiers returned to their villages local atrocities increased. Once again Dietrich made plans for the escape of the Kropotkins, but when he came to see them he was met with prevarication.

'There is some difficulty, some difficulty,' the Prince kept muttering.

Before Dietrich left the Princess came in and the mystery was solved. A spaniel was having puppies. They could not take her with them on a journey in such a condition or the puppies might die. Dietrich saw there was nothing else he could do but remarked, 'Is it not more important you live than the puppies die?'

She patted the dog, keeping her head down, pretending not to hear.

On the sixth of November the Bolsheviks took over. Kerensky fled. High winds and heavy snowstorms isolated Kolotovka. During the blanketed months Dietrich made a 'desperation plan' to meet changing circumstances. The whole estate, with the exception of the forest and fifty acres round the house, would be shared among the peasants. Large areas were to be retained for communal use until the young men came of age. Dietrich showed it to the Prince. He agreed.

The spring came. Things had changed. The efficient ruthlessness of Lenin had created workable structures. The Moscow Central Executive Committee was functioning and Regional Soviets had been established with unlimited local powers. The peace treaty was signed at Brest-Litovsk, a relief to Dietrich: his country was no longer fighting Russia. He thought with great care as to what his next step should be. As yet no interest had been shown by the Regional Soviet in Kolotovka. He decided to call at the headquarters in Saltykov and present his plan. The old man sat for three days from morning till night waiting in an ante-room, with peasants preferred to him again and again, before he was granted an interview by a young man of thirty with greasy black hair and a hooked nose who, glancing through his papers, and comprehending in a moment their gist, looked up and coldly asked two questions: 'Why did you not promote this scheme before? Is your employer a cousin of Pyotr Kropotkin?'

He made a note of Dietrich's replies and dismissed him with a nod, explaining that they would hear from him. His name was Leon Gorsky.

Dietrich returned reasonably optimistic and did not hide from the peasants his scheme to give more land to them and their children. One day he noticed men with measuring rods in the home meadows. An uneasy peace prevailed on the estate and the steady work of farming continued.

July was another month of rumours. The Czechs were approaching. The allies had landed in the north. The Tsar had escaped and then on the twenty-third came the news of the murder of the Imperial family. Prince Pavel was shocked, and, as the spaniel had recently whelped, suggested it might now be sensible to leave the country. But on the thirtieth of July, before new plans could be made, a letter was received addressed plainly to Pavel Dimitrich Kropotkin stating:

'Representatives from the Regional Soviet will visit Kolotovka on the first of August.'

Scrawled beneath the stark message was the signature 'Leon Gorsky'.

And so it came about that on the afternoon of the following hot day the Prince and Princess, Dietrich and old Anna stood grouped in a window facing the road, waiting for the visitation which would decide their fate. Prince Pavel did not speak. He seemed to be gazing with curious intensity at the road. Irena Petrovna was wearing her best dress of shot mauve silk, already five years old but as she only wore it on rare occasions, it looked brand new. She secretly hoped to keep it for her lifetime and avoid the trouble of travelling forty miles to order another. Perhaps her husband's silence made her nervous for she kept smoothing her skirt with her hand.

At last, irritated, he said gently, 'Be still, my dear,' and looked back at the road.

Dietrich stood between them with Anna hovering behind, and tried calmly to consider the likely result of the visit. Had they come to dispossess them? To carry them off to prison, to shoot him as an enemy alien? But surely the relationship with Pyotr Kropotkin must be remembered and, after all, for the last seventy years the peasants had been treated better at Kolotovka than anywhere else. Perhaps they had come to accept his plans! He was old and sometimes hardly cared what happened.

Prince Pavel pointed to a cloud of dust on the road moving slowly towards them. In a few moments they could see two vehicles. The first was a carriage with a hatless peasant in a smock sitting up front, while behind him could be made out two figures in dark clothes.

'Is it Pyotr Kropotkin coming to see us in our home?' asked Irena Petrovna.

'No,' said Dietrich, 'one is Leon Gorsky. I do not know the other but he is a young man.'

The second vehicle was larger, a cart of sorts, drawn by two stout horses. As it drew closer they could see it was filled with straw on which five men were lounging. Dietrich asked himself who they could be. Were they simply guards against the bandits in the forest? The vehicles passed out of sight towards the village. He looked at his watch. They should be with them in ten minutes. They watched and waited; nothing happened.

At last the Prince said, 'I do not know why these men have come but I am going to see,' and turning to his wife said, in a voice in which there was for the first time in his life a hint of command, 'Please stay with Dietrich.'

'Why do you leave me alone?' she wailed. He did not answer but kissed her before going out.

'Let us go upstairs,' she said, 'from there we can see what happens.'

Looking out of a top window they could see her husband walking up and down by the gate, possessed of an unusual energy. From the village came a little procession led by Gorsky, and another thick-set, resolute-looking man, suggesting a factory foreman. Behind them came five peasants from the village: Grigori who killed the ducks, Yermolai, Vaska the carpenter – a pupil of the Bavarian's – and two young men, Fomich and Mitya, followed by the five men from the cart, now carrying rifles, with bayonets fixed, slung loosely over their shoulders as they shambled along.

'Soldiers, have mercy on us!' the Princess cried, putting her hand to her mouth.

'Don't worry,' said Dietrich, 'officials cannot travel without guards through the woods.'

She stood biting her nails.

Gorsky and the other representative broke away from the others to shake hands. They talked for a minute or two and it seemed as if Prince Pavel was speaking of the occupants of the house for he half-turned, pointing his hand. The two men shook their heads and smiled. A decision had been reached. He opened the gate and pushed it wide for the party to pass through, himself waiting to shut it behind them.

Then something inexplicable happened. The five peasants clustered together for a moment and, without warning, and to the surprise of the soldiers who almost toppled over them, flung themselves on the ground at the Prince's feet. From the house they could see him standing erect, unmoving. But Gorsky who, to begin with, had stood rigid with surprise was suddenly galvanized into action. He took two huge jumping strides towards the prostrate peasants, leaned forward and made upward thrusting movements with his hands, ordering them to rise. They paid no attention. He stood exasperated, his hands on his hips. In their own time, still ignoring him, they stood up one by one, dusted themselves and in turn bowed low to the pale Prince who, as if dreaming, continued to stare over their heads. After the peasants and soldiers had passed through he carefully closed the gate and the whole party walked out of sight behind the great barn. The tension was broken. Dietrich wiped his brow.

'Thank goodness. That will show Gorsky – they have proved loyal to their Prince.'

'Oh, I must have some tea,' said Irena Petrovna. They went downstairs to the drawing room and she rang the bell. Nobody answered. Old Anna went and fetched them cups. They were sitting drinking when a commotion was heard at the back of the house, a noise of banging doors and heavy feet, unused to treading lightly, stamping down the passage. The door opened and Gorsky and the other representative came in without knocking, the rest jostling behind. Dietrich rose to his feet and the two women came together holding hands. Gorsky looked slowly round the room taking in the old prints, the bad ancestral paintings, the gilded tables and mirror, the draped table covered with knick-knacks. His face remained impassive but his companion, nervous, irritated, walked over to the side table and pushed a Chinese bowl on the floor. Gorsky paid no attention and asked coldly:

'Which of you is the wife of Pavel Dimitrich Kropotkin?'

Before she had time to answer Dietrich stepped forward and said in his shrill voice, 'Sir, we have met. I came to see you in Saltykov. May I ask why you have come in here and where is Prince Pavel?'

'You will see,' Gorsky replied in his detached voice. The second member of the Executive, wishing to assert himself, pushed forward and taking a bundle of notes from his pocket read, 'You are Herr Dietrich whom we have been informed is a German spy and countryman of the late Alexandra, mistress of the Priest Grigori Rasputin. Well, you will soon find out whether the harlot has gone up or down.'

He looked round for applause. Nobody laughed.

'And who,' said Gorsky, looking at Anna without interest, 'are you?'

She trembled and swallowed but seemed unable to speak.

'Huh, she's nothing,' said his companion, 'not worth bothering about. Now Herr Dietrich, if you would be good enough to escort the lady of the house by the arm, we will take her to her husband.'

He did as he was told, surprised at her courage. She was maintaining a trembling dignity. They walked out of the house, through the yard and turned behind the great barn where, stretched out by the wall, lying on his face, dark stains showing through the back of his coat, lay her thin husband. She gave a little sob, ran over and kissed him. Everyone except Gorsky seemed taken aback as, straining, she pushed and pulled the body until the dead face looked upwards. The skin was dirty but unmarked and he looked sad as usual. She bent down again, kissed the forehead and stood up, her little round red face wrinkled with disbelief, and gazed intently at the peasants to whom the soldiers had passed their rifles. She had loved two of them as children and loved the children of the other three. Her husband had educated them, given them land, paid for their illnesses – what unkindness had they ever shown them?

They started shuffling with embarrassment, her questioning gaze upsetting them. They mumbled something to each other, pushed back their rifles into the hands of the soldiers and, approaching the little woman, threw themselves at her feet in the same way as they had prostrated themselves before her husband.

'Oh, little mother,' said Yermolai, 'we wish to thank you for everything. You and the Prince gave us good houses and good land, education and health. We wish to thank you as we thanked him, so you can both go with our blessing.'

Vaska the carpenter chimed in, smiling at her apologetically as if trying to explain away a broken plate.

'You see, the new Government is our Government. They have told us to shoot you. It is not our wish and we would not until we had shown you both our respect, gratitude and love and commended you to God.'

They got up again, brushed the dust off their smocks and took the rifles back from the soldiers. Dietrich, following a wave from Gorsky's hand, walked over and bowed to the puzzled little woman. Both fell at the first irregular volley. She was shot through the heart but it took several jabs of the bayonets before the body of the fat old Bavarian ceased to move.

Then the party moved off to the little tavern – built twelve years beforc by Prince Pavel – to celebrate the end of the bad old days and the birth of a new system based on brotherly love, equality, justice and fair shares for all men.

Service

There were in 1888 few more beautiful houses in England than Highwood, the property of Lord Pewsey. It stood in the middle of a huge park ringed by woods of giant beeches above a winding lake across which two classical temples looked at each other. One, a graceful square block, designed by the younger Adam, was joined by a stone-pillared arcade topped with urns to another long, dignified unpretentious house surrounding two courtyards. To the west of this building stood the orangery and statue gallery.

Inside the central door of the latter, facing the box garden, a tea table had been prepared, with a silver tea-pot, a silver kettle beneath which a wick burned, and several plates of thinly cut sandwiches and cakes. From a door at the kitchen end of this gallery which extended through the whole western end of the 'small house' the butler, Kelly, emerged to inspect the tea table.

A tall, heavily-built Irishman whose black hair was only slightly touched with grey, he was, from Tuesday morning until midday Monday, the perfect servant. At midday Monday he quietly retired to his bedroom to get drunk. Undisturbed he was harmless; disturbed bellicose, and a powerful puncher. Lady Pewsey had once suggested to a dismayed vicar that he should call on Kelly one Monday evening to remonstrate with him. But to her surprise and the vicar's relief Pewsey had interrupted sharply, 'Oh Evie, don't meddle. He's honest, keeps the men in order and the silver in perfect condition, so what if he does drink a little Irish whiskey on Monday? He is cold sober the rest of the time and I hate change.'

Lady Pewsey had flushed, pursed her lips, but said nothing. She knew when Pewsey was not to be contradicted. Kelly was left alone.

Today he examined the tea table, the cleanliness of the cups, the height of the flame on the wick, the angle of the sugar tongs and, picking up a plate of thinly-sliced cucumber sandwiches, looked at them with a frown. The neat, overlapping rows of five were irregular. Six in one row and five in the others. He picked out the unwanted criminal and ate it, not that he liked cucumber but it was the tidiest thing to do. This action was noticed with delight by an old lady, still erect, dressed in black with a white mob cap and lace shawl, who had entered the gallery from the library end. Despite her seventy-eight years she walked silently and briskly. Her pure white hair, still thick, was parted in the middle and drawn back loosely behind her ears. Her brow was high, her eyes brown, large and far apart. Her nose, crooked, as she said rather than aquiline, her mouth large, generous and often smiling, her chin firm. She was a fine, handsome old woman and had certainly been a fine, handsome girl. But her personality transcended appearance. Kindness, humour, sense, good nature and above all, power, emanated from every line of her wrinkled face.

'Caught you, Kelly,' she said with delight, 'I'll write and tell Lady Pewsey you are eating all the best things before they reach me.'

Kelly smiled and bowed. They understood each other. She sat down facing the garden as he poured out her tea. She was, at seventy-eight, one of the great Victorian matriarchs. Thirteen of her own children had lived and she now had over one hundred grandchildren and approaching two hundred descendants. She was fond of, or interested in nearly all of them, the feared and loved link binding together numerous incompatible families.

Today Kelly noticed she was not herself. It must be to do with Lady Harriet's arrival. Slowly he said, 'Her Ladyship arrived on the three-thirty train and went upstairs to rest. She has been told tea is ready.'

She looked up quickly. How like the Southern Irish. They might be reckless and unreliable sometimes but they were sympathetic and understanding.

'Oh Kelly,' she said, 'you are a mind reader. Yes, if she has finished her sleep I would like to see her.'

When the butler had gone she stood up undecided, and walked a few paces down the gallery. Harriet had always been difficult. It was so much easier when children were obedient. She sighed, looking up at a huge Roman athlete, his body marred by a new white marble fig leaf. Really, she thought, smiling again, Evie is a fool to put on all these stupid leaves. After all, everybody knows what a man looks like. She herself had been brought up in one of the greatest Whig palaces in a less hypocritical age when nudity in art had never been concealed or mentioned. Now this ridiculous puritanical pretence. In her day women knew everything but never mentioned the unmentionable. Now they pretended to know nothing and never stopped drawing attention to their ridiculous modesty. Thank goodness Pewsey had put his foot down about over-painting parts of his pictures.

She walked across the box garden. Still she could not be angry with Evie. It was so nice of her and Pewsey to lease her Highwood during their five years in Canada. How beautiful it was looking over the lawn to the lake with the beech woods growing down to the water.

'Good afternoon, Mama,' said Harriet's voice behind her.

She jumped and turned round prepared to be pleased, but her daughter's insignificant, rather long, prim, plain face and cold manner made it difficult. However, she took both her hands and kissed her on both cheeks and, saying how nice it was to see her, walked, leaning on her arm, back to the tea table.

'Milk?'

'No thank you, Mama.'

'Sugar, surely?'

'No thank you, Mama.'

Oh dear, she thought, I am sure if I had given her plain tea she would have wanted both. Somehow it was typical of her to have neither. There was a silence. Harriet refused the sandwiches and cakes. Then she spoke.

‘You sent for me, Mama.’

‘Well, my dear child, I hoped you would come and see me.’

‘I can guess why. I don’t want to.’

‘Guess what, and don’t want to what?’ she said tartly, thinking her daughter had bad manners.

Harriet quailed and appeared to be fighting back tears as, dropping her eyes, she said softly, ‘To marry.’

‘What do you plan to do then?’

‘Mama, you know what I wanted and you would not let me, and now I don’t want to marry anybody.’

‘Harriet, what is the point of regretting the past? I could not let you marry a penniless younger son. You have very little money of your own. By now if you were anything like your sisters you would have twelve children and be in the poor house. Would you thank me for that?’

The conversation was going just as Harriet had feared. All her arguments sounding wise and convincing in the train, now seemed lightweight, silly. She felt herself shrinking, her mother slowly getting her way. She pulled herself together, trying to speak firmly. ‘But Mama, I have spoken to Katie, you know all the houses she has. Well, she says I can have rooms for three years at Wood Town in Sussex. They only go there for two months every summer and she would like me to be there to look after things, and the garden,’ she finished rather lamely.

Her mother sat silent for a moment. At last she said coldly, ‘Why do you think Henry would like you hanging about one of his houses like a genteel governess? No daughter of mine will embarrass her sister by demeaning herself. Now be quiet and I will tell you the advice my father gave me when I was eighteen and, like you, was in love with a uniform. Let me say you are the first of my daughters to whom I have had to relate this.’

She paused, and into her voice came the lingering, unconsciously plaintive tone of the old remembering past days when they lived, not observed, life. Her twisted fingers came out and held Harriet’s large, bony white hands, binding closer mother to daughter, weakening an already faltering resolve.

'It was, I remember, in Papa's library. I was sent for one evening after supper. His room was always blazing with the lights of dozens of candles. I was put in a large chair which stood in a corner. He dragged another up beside me and then, instead of sitting down, walked around snuffing the candles so I knew he was worried. When it was nearly dark he sat down and crossed his knees and looked me in the face.

' "Well, Beatrix," he said, "I hear you want to marry young Lister and I have to tell you why you cannot." Then he laughed and said, "Oh dear, I hate explanations, you know. But you see, love does not last in marriage and if you marry this boy you will be unhappy."

'I saw Papa was nervous. This stopped me from weeping and I listened, embarrassed to have upset him.

'He began, "Have you ever read Lord Chesterfield?" I still remember his face as he spoke. He astonished me – I did not even know who he was talking about.

' "No." I must have shown my surprise, for he smiled.

' "You ought to, you know, I've heard it said every gentleman should read him. In my opinion every girl should too, you know."

'Oh dear,' said the old woman, 'I cannot go on in his precise words, for he used "you know" at least twice in every sentence so in the nursery we called him "you know", a disrespectful nickname you see, like the one you all had for me.'

She laughed and squeezed Harriet's hand, who almost groaned at the way she was undermining her with sympathy, knowledge and affection.

' "Well then," Papa went on, "it is a book which tells the truth about human nature, how rank – although it is not a word I would use – and money are the aims and envies of mankind, their possession ensuring the advantages and pleasures of life, the keys to the great world. His letters are vulgar, but true. Unless you marry into a position equal to the one in which you were born you will find things change. This you will regret, and you who are and should remain an object for others to envy, will envy what you have lost. I know you think you are in love, which is what matters.

It is untrue. Love seldom survives a change of circumstances, and anyhow lasts only a few years. If you wish for happiness you must regard your life as a whole, the future as well as the present, not discard the advantages of influence and position for a momentary inflammation of the heart. These are personal reasons, against what you doubtless call 'your heart's choice'. There is another. You are aware, I am sure, although I have never mentioned the subject, that I am proud of the achievements of our family. Our original status, as you know, was gentle but modest, until a fortunate wind blew us into the Court of Henry VIII. The gift of my old home and many other Church lands was, it is said, the cause of a curse. If so, it was ineffective. As a family we have prospered, but in every branch we have put service to the people above service to the King. That is what we believed and believe to be correct and honourable. It cost us the head of perhaps our most noble ancestor and frequent withdrawals from Court, in one of which we farmed and drained a quarter of eastern England, turning water savages in two generations into rich Tory farmers.

' "My dear, you may well say what has this to do with you? To which I reply you have admirable qualities befitting a great position in life at a time when our beliefs, our authority, our possessions are threatened. Our enemy is not the old Tory but the new man, the enemy of the people, the working man who has risen above his own despised class and treats his fellow men as a drunken drover his horse, driving them towards revolution. In the past days we defended the working men against the King. It is now our duty as a class to defend him against himself. You cannot do so by tying yourself to an impecunious cavalry officer whose pleas I fear I must dismiss. I can inform you that Barleytown's godfather and trustee has discussed with your mother your marriage to his godson. His possessions are great, his character admirable, his future and that of his tenants is in your hands. You must consider now whether you should not please your parents from whom you have ever received love and attention and to whom you owe the duty of obedience. You should recognize our superior experience and sincerest wishes for your future happiness and, remember, women at eighteen are devoted to others, from twenty-five to forty-five to themselves, at fifty to their children. This is an inexorable rule of life transcending the misleading beliefs of youth. Go – I will not allow you to imprison yourself in poverty," he ended, pulling me by both hands off the chair and kissing me, "go and speak to your mother."

'Well, I cried a little for a week. But in six months I married Barleytown. I am proud of him. I have done all I could for him. I have influenced the rest of my daughters with my father's advice, which time taught me was wise. You cannot deny, my dear, their marriages have been blessed by children and success.'

'Bella,' murmured Harriet.

'Well yes,' and in the disconcerting way the old woman had of disarming, she burst into a fit of laughter. 'But Bella, my dear, is the silliest fool in England. Any wife who puts salts in her husband's closet and brays with laughter would drive any husband away. But remember her child will inherit his father's houses and she still has a position in society. The sillier you are the more important it is to marry well, otherwise you have nothing!'

Her mother laughed and gripped her hands. 'Dear Harriet, I know how sensible and modest you are. I know you don't think you need marry and all your little nephews and nieces will be enough for your old age. You are wrong,' she continued, with an upward look, a momentary pause and a studied avoidance of her daughter's flushed face. 'Your sisters, while of course loving you, have already begun to take advantage of you, to use you. Do not let it continue. Do not again go to stay with Louisa when in truth you are looking after her children while she goes to France. You may pretend you are not being used but you are beginning to be sent on with the luggage, and it will get worse. I know you see yourself living in a little wisteria-covered house at Windsor, never lonely because a beloved niece or great-niece will always be with you. They will not, you know. It is cruel to say so, it would be crueller not to, spinsters soon become jokes. Do not forget how heartless you were as children. Do not think younger generations will be any kinder. My dear, a single woman of fifty is laughed at and has no children to console her. Why put yourself in such a position? You are still handsome, only thirty-eight and can have a husband who will give you a nice place in Limerick, every summer in London, and your children equality with their cousins. Why not accept such advantages?'

She stared intently at Harriet who suddenly remembered how her brother always said, 'Mama is a witch you know, she knows what you think. And you do what she wants.'

Was she a witch? The little house at Windsor, the iron railing, the steps mounting above the little white-windowed basement. The great twisting wisteria always in her mind in flower, engulfing a red brick front. How silly it all seemed now, the wisteria dead, no loved nieces enjoying a daily walk up the great avenue. She remembered with a little gasp how Louisa had continually yawned the last time they talked. The cold truth of her mother's words penetrated and chilled her. Her future contracted. She saw herself an unwanted old spinster, sitting alone before an empty grate, knitting something nobody wanted.

She got up to stop herself bursting into tears. Her mother rose at the same time and, stepping sideways, flung open her arms, calling out in a compelling, tender voice, 'Harriet, my darling little silly. Do you remember how I used to call you that?' She hugged her daughter, whose heaving head now rested on her shoulder. 'Do not think I mean to be horrid or I do not love you. I just want you to be happy and you won't be if you try and ignore the world and dream.'

She lifted up her head and kissed her on the forehead, then stroking her hair, said, 'Now my darling, run away and dry your eyes and make yourself handsome for dinner. Lady Summertown is coming down with her son. I have never seen him but I understand he is forty-two, quiet, nice, kind and easy. If you marry him, breeding like we do, you will have a son. And lasting as we do you will live happily for forty years.'

Harriet cheered up a little, and as she walked slowly, weakly back to her room decided with reluctance that it was her duty to obey her mother.

She had a son eighteen months later and in fact lived only for another thirty-nine years. In her old age she told her grandchildren always to take their mother's advice if they wished to be happy. She had, and never regretted it. But they were sick of the endless stories of Grandmother and secretly thought her a silly, snobbish old fool. All of them ignored her advice and made unhappy marriages for love.

La Gioconda

Helen lay for some time half awake, motionless in one of those early morning limbos which can either turn to sleep or consciousness. At last, becoming aware that she was not in her own bed she looked at her watch, saw it was very early and, jumping out of bed, ran with three strides to the window and looked at the rising sun lightening the sky. She could see dew on the grass and the air smelt fragrant, of Italian earth, thyme and olives. Standing on tiptoe she stretched her arms, clenching and unclenching her beautiful hands. Feeling satisfied, ready for the day, she leaned further out looking westwards to the steep, ilex-covered hills which fell towards the villa. A mist was rolling down with surprising speed.

The exciting thought came to her to run up the avenue and meet it, to bathe in its fragrant coolness. She felt positively pagan. Her mind made up, she turned away from the window, passing the bed where her husband lay fast asleep, walked through the drawing room and down the steps. Now she could see the mist had already obscured the end of the avenue. Quickly she ran to meet it, her bare feet chilled by the dew. Yet how sensual was the momentary softness of the prickly sun-baked grass. She met the mist halfway up the avenue and threw both hands up in an open embrace as the two came together.

She walked on feeling deliciously cool, the moisture settling on her, making her luxuriant hair heavy, caressing her body; again she stretched herself to her utmost height and went and sat on a wall. There was something secret, exciting, to be alone in such a confined, secret place, helpless. How fitting if the great god Pan or a centaur were now to appear. They must have lived in places such as these where the forests stretched unending for miles. She got off the wall and lay on the prickly ground examining her long, slim arms and legs, her flat stomach and jutting breasts. She longed for adventure, for one of the wood gods to loom out of the mist demanding the sacrifice of her beauty. She lay back, expectant, but nothing happened. A beetle crawled over her back. Angry, she stood up and walked back to the house.

The mist had thickened now, you could only see a few yards, so it gave her quite a fright when a figure suddenly appeared. It was only old Carlo, the gardener, crossing the avenue on his way to clean the swimming pool. Had he been following her, she wondered? He gave her such a peculiar look before quickly turning his back. Goodness, she hoped he was not going to fall in love with her. Desiring Pan was one thing, but playing Lady Chatterley with Carlo was quite another. But he had given her an odd look, although, of course, so many men stared at you in Italy. It could have been only innocent admiration.

She climbed the steps and, before going into the house, ran her hands over her body, satisfied at the hard feel of a well-trained racehorse. Still reluctant to go in, she put her hands behind her thick, lustrous hair and, noticing it was covered with the minutest drops of water, ran the gleaming braids through her fingers and tossed her head back. At the same time she hoped Carlo wouldn't mention her nakedness, for her hosts, William and Rowena, were getting on, and the old were always jealous of the young and beautiful.

In their bedroom Hugh was still fast asleep, lying on his back snoring. She stood looking down on his beaky, aquiline nose, the receding bottom half of his face, where a weak chin was concealed by a red beard. Even in sleep he looked as if he were missing his glasses. Poor man, she knew he found it difficult to live up to her, but she was not the first beautiful woman to be tied to a man unable to appreciate her finer points. In a way his laziness and indolence were useful. He never seemed to know or care whether she had lovers. Perhaps it was because he realized no man should have such loveliness to himself, but how typical of him to be asleep when she came back passionate, a child of nature, covered in mist and dew. It lowered her spirits, made her anxious to regain her confidence by standing in front of the long mirror looking at herself. How romantically her reflection stared back, how startlingly green even the early morning light showed her eyes. The pleasure of seeing them made her relax, give her famous smile, her lips shaping into that enigmatic, mysterious curl which had once made some poor fool of a gossip columnist refer to her as La Gioconda, without realizing the insult of the comparison. But she was incredibly, mysteriously beautiful.

Once again she ran her hands over her firm body then, with a quick movement, put them behind her shoulders and threw forward her great mane of black hair, leaving her standing in the dark under her own waterfall. She parted the cascade a little in front and looked to see if the pose was effective. Suddenly she was interrupted by 'good morning, darling', followed by a request to know what she was doing. She stood motionless, unanswering. God, how prosaic Hugh was. How dull to hear his flat tones, to be conscious of being peered at through pebbled spectacles as she stood there, naked, unappreciated, with the lustre of morning on her, fresh from dancing in the loving view of Pan. For she had heard hooves impatiently pawing at the ground, sensed hard, cruel, loving eyes fixed on her in desire, had resisted the call to the woods, the escape over fallen branches, cruel stones and unknown paths to be thrown under some great ilex tree on a pile of moss and taken cruelly, her nostrils full of the acrid smell of his lust.

She had refused, to come back instead to Hugh sitting up in bed, peering at her, taking the first puffs of his morning cigarette and starting on an unfinished *Daily Telegraph* puzzle. How banal he was, how sad she had to walk alone with the gods. Of course, she would never leave him, it would be sentencing him to death, but sometimes she despised him, pitied him for his mundane tedium. Oh why, when she came back with the savagery of the woods about her, couldn't he jump out of bed and take her as she was? She would have taught him what love could mean. Instead he looked up and said, 'Salamis was sea-born, wasn't it?'

In reply, she slammed the door on the way to the bathroom.

Hugh didn't pay much attention and quietly continued with his puzzle. When she came back she thought how tired he looked. Everything about him seemed to droop, his hair, even his beard, and he was so short. I must be nice to him, she thought, and lay on her stomach, her chin on her hands, fixing her beautiful green eyes on his face.

'Darling Hugh,' she said, a trifle desperately, 'I *am* lucky to have you, I realize that.'

'Thank you, darling.'

'But there's one thing we must discuss – the little girls are being tiresome.'

'The girls? How?'

She thought deeply before replying. 'Well, you see, they are starting to interrupt me and it's silly at their age because nobody wants to listen to them. What's more, I think they hate me.'

'The girls?'

'Yes, Hugh, the little girls, and please don't go on repeating exactly what I say. You must know what I'm talking about.'

'But they love you and you are always telling them to talk.'

'Yes, but not to interrupt and they have picked up the irritating habit of telling my stories as if they were their own.'

Hugh was silent. She watched him carefully, uncertain whether he was on her side.

Then he said quietly, 'What do you want me to say?'

She spoke hysterically. 'Tell them not to interrupt, not to talk all the time after dinner, and, when I am with somebody else, not to come between us, and especially not to go out without asking. Can't they understand that they are children and must keep quiet and do what they are told?'

Hugh said in a weary voice, 'All right, I will see them, but let us have breakfast first, you must be tired after your early morning walk.'

The children had finished breakfast and Hugh, not finding them in the house or garden, eventually discovered that some new friends had called and taken them to the sea for a picnic. They would not be back until the evening.

When he told Helen she flew into a rage and, stamping her feet, shouted 'Really, what will they do next? You must insist they ask me before they do it again, they could be killed or kidnapped. Anything could happen to children of that age.'

Then, exhausted, she went and slept while Hugh sat under a tree and read a book until the butler told him at a quarter to twelve that drinks would be on the upper terrace in half an hour as guests were expected. He went to change and wake Helen who, cheered by the idea of strangers, prepared herself, for she was bored without company.

The guests turned out to be distant cousins, a shy couple who lived most of the time in the country in England, except for the summer months when they had a house in the hills nearby. Helen was at her best with Frederick Henderson. She knew every sort of story about his father and mother and uncles so he must have felt grateful and at ease to be so welcome. Rowena, too, must have been delighted at his subjection. She did not have a moment to be bored by him at lunch, so thoroughly was he entertained. Helen retired for her siesta at half past three in a triumphant mood, the perfect guest.

That evening Hugh was reading again under his favourite tree when a car drew up, the laughter and banging of doors telling him that the children were back. Putting his book down with some reluctance and making a wry face, he decided to talk with them now, otherwise they might upset Helen again at dinner. Slowly he walked towards their bedroom in the guest house, and from outside saw them lying laughing on their beds. He walked in and asked if they had enjoyed their day. They both jumped up, kissed him and said yes, it had been lovely. Annabel had swum a whole mile out to sea and Jane half as far.

Then there was a moment's silence and Hugh said, 'My darlings, you know how much your mother loves you, but she is not altogether happy at the moment. In fact she is rather upset because she says you both interrupt her.'

Annabel who was nineteen, and Jane who was eighteen, looked at each other and started to laugh hysterically before bursting into tears.

'What is it?' said Hugh, getting up and going over and kissing them. They put their arms around his neck without saying anything. 'What is it?' he asked again.

'Mummy,' Annabel suddenly burst out, 'it's Mummy. We can't bear it any longer. We will get jobs as waitresses or something, but we are definitely leaving. If we don't speak she says we are shy, if we do we are childish. Oh, Daddy, can't you see, she's ruining our lives? She won't even let us use make-up or go out alone, and if our friends come to see us she talks her bloody head off and treats us as children and, and, . . . we have even caught her kissing Tom and . . .' She pulled herself up. 'It makes us look like idiots,' and she started sobbing again.

Hugh, perfectly distraught, got up and paced up and down. Then Annabel nudged Jane to tell her it was her turn. She tried to speak reasonably, 'Can't you see, Daddy, how ghastly it is to have to see one's own mother sunbathing topless when, honestly . . . and wearing bikinis which, well . . . don't suit her, and then, and then the other day she sunbathed nude in front of all our friends. Oh, oh, oh . . .'

The two girls clung to each other wailing. Poor Hugh put his hands over his eyes and felt like joining them.

Jane came and knelt by him and said, 'Oh Daddy, I'm so sorry, but can't you see Mummy's madly jealous of us and that it's much better if we go away. Henry left six years ago, and Alec three, and they get on fine now when they see her.'

'Yes,' said Annabel, 'it's best we should go without a row, but it's up to Mummy. I won't stand being talked to like a child again. The rest of our time here we are going to do exactly what we like, see who we want, say what we think and put on what make-up we want to. Now go, go,' they said suddenly, both pushing him, 'and tell her while you are still on our side, otherwise you never will. You know how kind you are.'

Hugh found Helen in the drawing room, rearranging some

flowers which had been perfectly arranged but were now all over the table and floor. Something about his face frightened her; surely he had not gone over to the children? Was everyone going to turn on her? Panic seized her and she took a step backwards. Hugh saw her fear and went and held her, telling her it was impossible for the girls to come out of the shadow of so beautiful a mother and, unless they were allowed to go away and stand on their own feet they would never develop. So, for her sake and theirs they should leave. Helen was not placated. Somehow she sensed the unity her husband and children had reached in the guest house. It made her feel old, tired, and when she put her hand to her head the lustrous tresses which had slipped through her fingers that morning had turned to a mop of dead, wiry hair.

'Oh, I hate you all,' she gasped, 'how I hate you. For years I stuck to you and came back to you, when hundreds of people loved me; but I was too kind to leave you and now you turn on me.'

She ran to her room, locked the door and lay down on the bed. 'Oh,' she thought, as she kicked the mattress with her bandy little legs, 'Oh God, I'm nearly fifty, my body sags, my skin is like old paper, there is nothing to do but die, so I shall, quickly, and let them see how they get on without me. It will teach them a lesson.'

The idea of how they would suffer pleased her. She sat up and wiped away the mascara, lipstick and rouge which had mixed and congealed in the most unexpected places and colours on her face and the pillow.

Hugh came and rattled on the door, calling her. She refused to answer and he went away. How miserable he must be, she thought with satisfaction as she cleaned her face. Then a thought struck her. Perhaps he was not the fool he looked, perhaps it would be wiser for the girls to go away, to have a flat in London and work. It was well known that beautiful mothers had resentful children. Perhaps it was true that the girls were difficult because they were so jealous. Presently she felt she had done enough face-cleaning and it was time to make herself beautiful again. Getting out her little brushes, eye black, rouge, two shades of powder, mascara and lipstick, she started all over again. As she looked at her beautiful green eyes in the mirror she thought that even if Hugh was right he needed teaching a lesson, so tomorrow at dawn she would go again into the mists of the ilex wood and, when she heard the faint pipings of Pan, the impatient pawing, she would not ignore them, but leap into his arms and cling to him as he leapt over cruel rocks until she was tossed into his soft bed of moss.

Her spirits had risen now and she continued quickly to make up her face. The light in the room was bad, perhaps she was not getting everything in exactly the right place but, anyhow, carelessness had always been a part of her wild appeal. In the darkening room Helen continued to look triumphantly into the mirror. Then, unlocking the door, she walked down the passage into the drawing room, taking in at a glance the little separated whispering groups and Rowena's sudden surprised, relieved smile. But she felt triumphant again, generous, forgiving. It would be kind to set their fears at rest. Giving the room an all-embracing dazzling smile she called out gaily, 'Goodness, I am famished. Is dinner ready?'

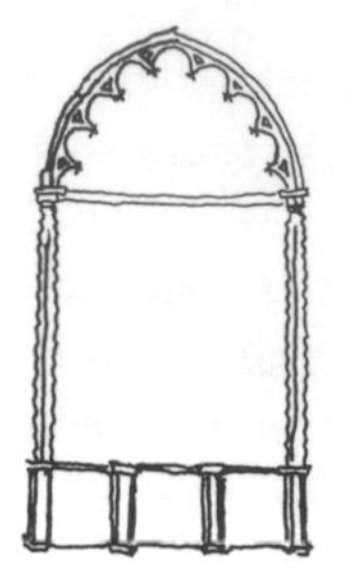

The Lunette

I

One morning in the month of May, in the early 1890s, two horse-drawn vehicles set out at varying times to journey from Siena to the little hill town of Montessa, some thirty kilometres away. The first to start, a dray, drawn by two stout bay horses, left the stable opposite the Fonte Branda before the sun had risen, loaded with two Florentines, a heavy black metal box and two large packages carefully packed in reams of brown paper secured with ropes beneath a waterproof tarpaulin. The second, a light travelling carriage, moved off from the door of the largest hotel on the Via Roma at precisely eight o'clock.

The black paint of the bodywork was spotless, the brass on the leatherwork glinted, the horses' coats shone like satin. The reins of this smart conveyance were held by a little groom of crooked and indefinite shape. A fustian coat extended to his fingertips, his breeches separated only a little above the knees, the brown leather encasing bow-legged calves shone brilliantly. A toothless, nut-brown face peeped out from under a brown bowler hat so large that, stuffed with brown paper, it hung without contact around his little wizened head like the eaves of a house. He never spoke, but marked even the smallest movement of the reins with a confidential hiss as if conversing with his horses in a secret language.

Behind him, on the right hand side of the carriage, sat a young Italian guide, Mario Franco, in every way a contrast. Twenty-four years old, he gave at first sight an impression of well-being. His black hair was thick and glossy, his complexion florid, full red lips gleaming between rounded protruding cheeks enclosing perfectly white teeth. A close-fitting coat buttoned up to the neck was worn above trousers tight, rounded and immaculate. His new gloves were of startling knitted yellow string. Every now and then he looked at some part of his apparel with lively satisfaction, not evident in the glances he nervously cast out of the corners of his eyes at the hirer of the carriage, Mr Bronson, a neatly dressed little man who sat erect beyond a large folded umbrella with a rug carefully wrapped around his legs against the chill morning air. He was one of those men whose faces make it difficult to judge his age or nationality. But Mario continued to observe him out of the corners of his eyes with intense interest. Although young, he considered himself a good judge of character, how else could he be the youngest Sienese guide or rather, courier, as he now termed himself on the thick, white, black gothic-lettered cards in his pocket-book. It was his invariable habit quickly to sum up his clients, estimating how much was to be made out of them.

To begin with, Mr Bronson had made a favourable impression. His neatly clipped moustache and beard, well-cut tweed cape, brown homburg and gold and pearl tie-pin all suggested money. Now Mario was uncertain; the eyes, deep-set beneath curved eyebrows, made him feel young and big-footed, while below the fine-boned, slightly aquiline nose the tightness of skin where the protruding middle of his nostrils pulled the nose down on to the upper lip reminded him unpleasantly of a Sienese money-lender of whom he did not wish to think. The mouth was thin-lipped, cut in stone. Nor was it reassuring to hear him enunciating words in precise, perfect Italian, suggesting competence and a worldliness antipathetic to profit. There was something else: Mario, looking at him sitting in the carriage, instinctively knew underneath the veneer of gentility and elegance the man was not a gentleman. Some indefinable instinct he had never felt before reached out and comprehended a background of European poverty not dissimilar to his own. His disappointment increased. In that case, they would understand each other only too well.

It was one of those bright mornings in central Italy when summer comes galloping out of spring. The oaks, as yet without leaves, appeared to be reaching up with renewed vigour, the poplars growing on the side of the rivulet at the bottom of the hill had already exploded into yellow-green leaf, every heavy, slowly swaying yellow branch bursting with life. The sunlight filtering through the trees illuminated the young dew-covered grass to a green so vivid that Bronson, leaning forward, appeared to hold his breath. Mario wondered what he was looking at, surely he had seen young grass before. He did not dare speak and they travelled on for a mile or so while he fidgeted in silence, then, unable to control himself any longer, '*monastero*', he said, pointing up the hill to the left of the road at a large red castellated building. Bronson turned his head, his eyes telling Mario 'do not speak until I speak to you', but he said nothing and looked back at the building, wondering would his offer be accepted? If so, to whom would he resell? He smiled, remembering his anger with Mrs G. last month. He had written to say he had found, in perfect condition, unrestored, uncleaned, a Giovanni di Paoli. She had replied by post-card, 'No, I have one.' Immediately he had started a letter suggesting that she think again, reminding her that 'collecting pictures was not collecting stamps'. Soon he had put down his pen. She would not stand correction, and was and could be kind and useful. He would have to bargain elsewhere, presenting himself as a salesman to those with whom he desired equality. He knew he was unnecessarily annoyed, the picture would sell, he would make twelve hundred pounds.

It was no good, he was upset again, all his appreciation of the beauties of the morning faded. Turning his eyes from the monastery he closed them, sighing, knowing the symptom only too well, the slipping without the power to resist, into one of those sloughs of despond into which he had fallen so often in the last few years. He never knew what little incident would bring on these dark moods. It did not help that he understood the underlying causes of his weary internal dissatisfaction; he could, or rather would, do nothing about them. Today his mood was not bad, he felt no despair, only depression and withdrawal from his surroundings. It was as if a blight settled on his thoughts, blanketing his appreciation of the loveliness of the morning, dulling his hopes.

The village of Santa Rosa lay at the entrance to one of the passes through the hills surrounding Siena. Mario was perplexed when they drove down the road through steep hills covered with ilex trees. The look Bronson had given him, the subsequent silence, was discouraging. Somehow he must display his talents to the rich American. It was an ideal opportunity to foster his emigration plans. What bad luck to strike an emigrant, or at best the son of one. Yet, if Bronson had emigrated and made good, might he understand? Mario sighed; how difficult it all was. But he had faith and determination to show his culture and knowledge. He could not forget his mother had come home last night with an ecstatic look, declaring with breathless excitement how, as she prayed at the altar of St Catherine, the saint had smiled, looked down and murmured in a gentle voice tomorrow her son would meet a rich, kind, helpful man. Of course; his mother was a fool, but he remembered a teacher saying fools were often inspired by the word of God. He felt elated, his spirits recovered, looking round he saw opportunity was near.

The small rough road on which the carriage was bowling along ran along the side of a ravine, to the right of a small, winding, stony river. A little further on it had once crossed the water by an old disused bridge. Now it continued on the right bank. Rounding a corner, the ruin came into sight. Mario leaned forward and touched Mr Bronson lightly on the arm, saying: 'Over that bridge, many centuries ago, Maria Pia was exiled by her husband to the Maremma. As she crossed over, she looked back and said "Siena . . ." .'

Mr Bronson, awoken as if from a dream, drew back his arm as if from a scorpion; and imperiously lifting his bony white forefinger, enunciated in a clear voice with a look of surprised pleasure:

Siena me fe' disfecemi Maremma
Salsi colui che'nnellata
Dispos andu m'aver con la sua femma*

He paused, surprised, embarrassed at this display of vulgar erudition he would have looked down on in another man, then he felt a shock of pleasure, his depression had magically lifted. He looked around like a man saved from drowning and gave Mario a gentle, grateful smile, thanking him for his information. The sudden change of mood made Mario almost fall back with surprise, for what utterly astonished him was the unconscious caress in Bronson's voice. He had spoken in tones which Mario himself used when he was anxious to convince a silly girl he loved her. His spirits rose, madmen may do anything, and his companion's good mood was confirmed by the way the little man now looked about. Instead of sitting slumped in sad thoughts he was now leaning forward; sideways, gazing with the same rapt interest he had looked at the sun on the grass beneath the poplars in the early morning. Again Mario followed Bronson's eyes; again, bewildered, shrugged his shoulders. What was interesting about young chestnuts breaking into bud, or the bright yellow broom creeping beneath them, or a single cypress, isolated, stark on a hill-top against the blue sky? He could show Bronson a hundred such cypresses.

Unconsciously he relapsed into his own favourite day-dream, imagining himself as an American millionaire, living in a large white house surrounded by a pillared verandah, set in green lawns, with numerous black servants. Every morning his beautiful blonde young wife would kiss him goodbye, every evening they would sit on the porch in easy chairs, his mother on his other side, dressed just like Queen Victoria, and both women would listen with admiration as he told them . . .

He was startled out of this pleasant reverie by Mr Bronson

* Siena saw my birth, Maremma my death, as well he knows that gave me his ring in holy matrimony.

leaning forward and tugging sharply at the old groom's coat, asking him in a sharp voice to stop the carriage which pulled up beside a broken gap in a wall, through which could be seen a bare, trodden space fronting a tumbledown wooden hut from which a barefooted farmboy had released a gaggle of geese. Free from confinement the birds waddled close together, nudging each other at every step, necks extended, hissing with excitement, occasionally pausing to stand on tiptoe and shake their wings. Bronson continued to stare, surely he had noticed something. Yes, there it was again, visible for a second before the shaking stopped, the upthrust wings showed curved bones at the joint, resembling a gothic arch, identical to countless angels' wings in Trecento pictures. How often had he thought artificial and architectural this frequently repeated joint! Here was the precise source. He gave a little shiver of elation: when the artist avoided nature and divorced art from his surroundings, he separated himself from the creation of those life forces which governed mankind, losing a comprehension of the whole which alone could convey tactility.

Happy, in tune with nature, he looked about him as they turned off the main road and wound their way into the hills ringing Montessa. The sun, hot for a spring day, beat down on the carriage as they slowly climbed. Bronson, feeling the heat at the back of his neck, turned, pointed to the umbrella and asked Mario with a smile to keep the sun off. The response was reluctant: it seemed to Mario undignified to treat a man in his position, with his knowledge, as a servant while ignoring his advice. He lifted the umbrella, but in such a way that the sun continued to fall on the back of the little man's head. Bronson turned and looked at him for a second and smiled. At once, Mario moved it to the correct angle. Maddened, despite his resolution to assert his personality, how quickly he obeyed the little man's look.

Soon they came to a division of road and a vast view fell away before them. Again the carriage was stopped and Bronson, getting out, stood erect, gazing westwards. The view was conventionally magnificent, range upon range of hills extending beyond the great valley to an horizon of dim peaks scarcely visible in the haze. He nodded as if in agreement with his memory. There was about the country a sense of monotony, a spiritual emptiness explaining why in all that huge expanse there were so few works of art. There were two pictures, he thought, at Radicondoli, to the south. But if you looked west, you could look over mountain and valley till you came to the sea without finding anything of interest. No scarcity of people caused this vacuum. What could be emptier than the desert south of Siena, yet there, in nearly every village, were things of loveliness. He would never forget how, on his first visit to Italy, rounding a bend, and seeing the red buildings of Monte Oliveto, growing out of the hill-top surrounded by countless cypresses, he had fainted, blinded by such beauty. Now he looked coldly at this landscape, deciding beauty was only to be found in the unexpected.

At eleven o'clock, they arrived at the base of the hill dominated by the stone crown of Montessa. As they started the ascent, Bronson decided to walk and, much to Mario's annoyance, the pair, united by the umbrella into a black-headed quadruped, climbed sedately until they neared the open gate. On reclimbing into the carriage Bronson, producing from a little leather bag a mirror, comb and handkerchief, repaired the damages of their promenade. Mario, mopping his brow with a large handkerchief, closed the umbrella and replaced it between them.

They drove through a crumbling arch into the little town, and up to the door of the church, its campanile and great stone carved door dominating the little square and the surrounding streets like a sitting chicken her young. Bronson was pleased to see the dray empty and the two horses munching contentedly at their nosebags, in the shade. To his satisfaction he also saw the two men he had brought from Florence, standing aloof with a detached air of authority.

On the ground stood a large black metal box with various metal protrusions. Its like had never been seen in the little town, and was creating intense interest among one of those small groups of men and women who appeared in those days as if by magic when anything of interest occurred to break the monotony of their lives. The old groom gave a hiss, the carriage stopped dead and Bronson climbed down and walked over to a fat priest who quickly distanced himself from the little group staring intently at the black box. He shook him by the hand and quickly pretended to blow his nose to wipe off the clamminess of the fat, red, hairy fingers. He was pleased, everything had gone well. The packages had been taken into the church; the black box waited. Relieved not to be angry with men who always insisted on doing things their own way, he looked up at the façade of the church, and his face, which had set at the touch of the priest's damp hand into a mould of repelled rigidity, softened at the sight of the carved stone door surrounding the two Etruscan remains, the ascending Pisan arches in the campanile, the fragmented Gothic rose window, all overlaid by seventeenth-century restoration, creating in its confusion an unconscious entity so often lacking in pure architecture.

Mario, noticing the change of expression, gave a little sigh of satisfaction and thought, perhaps he is not a swine, maybe if I can get him into the right mood he will help me to go to America. Bronson, as if in a trance, continued to stare at the church front, until one of the men from Florence came up and asked for instructions relating to the metal box.

Bronson spoke to him in a quiet voice and then, with a little bow to the priest, walked towards the main door. Mario, determined to miss nothing, followed like an oversized shadow. The little crowd looked at each other and, pressing even closer together, surged behind. The church, with its single nave, transept, apse, and two side chapels, had a forlorn air. The frescoes had faded into vagueness, in places obliterated by dark green mould which shafts of sunshine, glinting through the broken tiles of the roof, illuminated into the brilliance of polished malachite. Bronson, having lowered his eyes to accustom them to the gloom, turned to the Gothic arch in the west wall of the nave. There, exactly as he remembered, vibrant and angry, on the edge of his Gothic arch stood Ranieri in his flowing gown and little cap, his pride and petulance unaffected by six hundred years. Bronson stood still, reliving his delight at finding two years ago, in this little isolated hill town in the Maremma, a statue conceived in 1300 without relation to the classical or Gothic: dateless, the first realistic portrait of the Renaissance, unaffected by what had been or what was to come; a strange artistic island, its realism almost matched by the bishop tumbling out of his tomb across the nave.

No such thoughts pleased or troubled the priest and the little crowd, who started to fidget. What was this strange little man doing, staring lost in thought at what they had seen all their lives without a glimmer of pleasure or interest? Their shuffling and whispering eventually reached Bronson. He looked around to see where he was, then led his sheep across the transept to the Ranieri chapel.

Here the party was met by a huge young man twisting a battered brown stove-pipe hat, relic of many generations of christenings. Behind him stood a plump young woman, with a little boy trying to hide under her dress, and a newborn baby in her arms. The young man moved towards the priest, who made an angry gesture of dismissal, but Bronson gave him a bow and a small smile as they passed into the chapel where the local blacksmith with his little apprentice, almost hidden by a large leather apron, were putting into place above the altar a painting, the largest package from Florence. With a final tap of his hammer the blacksmith finished, climbed off his ladder and joined the little group looking up. There was a long, embarrassing silence.

At last, Bronson spoke in a detached, almost amused tone. 'It has, I am afraid, taken eighteen months to clean; it was in bad condition. I hope you are pleased.'

His listeners continued to look up with the absolute blankness of those who have no idea what to think or say. Perhaps, Bronson thought, it was not unreasonable, the chapel was dark, the sun had gone in, the restored painting was scarcely more than an association of shadows.

He continued bowing to the priest: 'I hope you will forgive me if in your church I take advantage of modern science to show your masterpiece as it should be seen.'

The priest nodded, not daring to speak. To save his life he could not remember what the battered picture Bronson had taken away eighteen months ago, looked like. He was terrified that a question would show his ignorance, but, to his relief, he soon ceased to be the centre of interest.

The two men from Florence came pushing callously through the crowd, every movement showing the contempt of the townsman for the peasant. One of them carried a large piece of machinery attached to a long, T-shaped piece of metal which, together, they held up in front of the picture, and looked round.

'Are you ready?' said Bronson.

The men nodded. A lever was pulled, followed by a hissing noise and, slowly, as if by magic, a brilliant harsh light illuminated the chapel. The infant Jesus was seen lying on the floor of the manger, at the feet of a large, brown, round-eyed cow. Before the pair, splendid in scarlet, blue and gold, the three wise men bowed. Uninterested, the Virgin gazed with a passive, calm expression. Beneath her chair was written in letters clear for the first time in four hundred years: 'This painting was made by Andrea Di Nicola in 1493.'

The brilliant light caused the priest's mouth to fall open, the petrified audience to crowd together, and the little boy to cry, hiding his face in his mother's skirt. The priest was the first to recover, remembering at last, revelling in the bright colours, congratulating himself on bringing back this glory to his church. Bronson looked with interest at the peasants, who huddled closer together, their faces ghastly in the flare lights, their mouths open with amazement. During the period between 1300 and 1600 the same faces, the same expressions, had stared out of countless backgrounds.

His thoughts were interrupted, as the priest, puffed out with pleasure like a frog, and groping unsuccessfully for his hands, gasped, 'Beautiful, beautiful, we owe you so much.'

'No,' he said, speaking precisely, 'I have been pleased to help you, but you will notice one ill side-effect of the cleaning, for while the painting is now as it should be and the painting of the predella is still bright, the lunette is blackened beyond repair. The contrast is disagreeable.'

'Yes,' said the priest looking up, his voice quavering. 'So it is.'

'But,' Bronson continued, 'although it is now reduced to a dark shadow, is no longer a painting, is valueless as a work of art, I still like it because of its association with this chapel.'

He paused, and Mario wondered why he was embarrassed.

'So I had another lunette painted which, if you wish – and it is for you to decide – I will exchange for this faded old thing. If your blacksmith will momentarily replace your picture by mine, you can judge.'

The flare faded, the blacksmith and the boy busied themselves in the dusk, the men from Florence remained isolated. The replacement was made.

In the still darkened chapel, Bronson continued in his precise tones: 'The new picture is in the style of Matteo di Giovanni, to whom the fragments of the original have been attributed. Will you please turn up the light.'

The gas flared, again the peasants huddled, while the priest gave a loud gasp of pleasure. There, in all its brightness and savagery, every detail vivid, gleamed the favourite subject of the Sienese: the Massacre of the Innocents. King Herod, a proud arm extended, sat exultant, satisfied at the pleasant scene, the soldiers' swords shone brightly, the distracted mothers, dressed in the height of fashion, sobbed, the blood of the infants glowed liquid red. The priest was ecstatic. Could the lunette be permanently fixed at once? If so, a hundred candles would see the chapel was never dark again.

'Yes,' said Bronson looking at his watch, it could be done in the next two hours while he rested.

He was tired, he would be grateful for the use of the priest's spare bed and a glass of water. That was all he needed. He had his sandwich box with him. They would start back at two-thirty.

II

When Bronson woke up, he knew by the heaviness of his spirits that the depression had returned. He hardly looked up, avoided shaking hands when the priest gratefully said goodbye and, as the carriage passed out of the gate, sank back in a little heap on the carriage seat. He hated himself on these occasions, the procuring and bargaining bruised his feelings and conflicted with his inner idealism, a youthful relic that lingered on in his mind, a personal religion unaffected by betrayals and the realism of his ambitions.

In youth he had been awakened by teachings among the dreaming spires of Oxford, which had grafted themselves to his yearning soul. Yet here he was, sitting in a carriage, returning from a visit to a little town where he had obtained, by methods he could not condone, a long-lost painting which, cleaned and restored, varnished and shining, he would sell to some American who would never receive from it a fraction of the pleasure it had given him, covered by the dirt of the centuries, in an old neglected church. Would he ever escape the bitter belief, that if he had been born in more fortunate circumstances he could have maintained untouched his idealism? As it was he had to make money, not for vulgar uses, but to avoid the servitude of dependence and achieve his obsession: a villa in the hills of his beloved Florence, where, surrounded by beautiful possessions, he would teach. Who should blame him escaping his past; the stark poverty of his early youth, beyond the pale of Estonia, the stink of the crowded boat sailing to the United States, the squalor of the small house in Boston his father had shared with three other families, the contempt of his school fellows. He had not been by nature ambitious for power.

His first plan was to be a philosopher, another William James, living simply, but an unforgettable day changed his life. His art master had taken three boys of promise to view one of the city's new Renaissance palaces. A stately English butler led them down long passages into a dark library lined with vellum and leather-bound books. He would always remember hearing the words: 'Mr Harold Bronson,' enunciated in clear English. How different and important it made him sound. Their host, Mr Terence O'Neill, put down his quill, pushed back his chair and, letting his pince-nez dangle on a black silk cord, shook hands with them in turn, expressing pleasure at their visit. He conducted them courteously around the house, progressing through rooms with magnificent stone fireplaces, tapestries and gleaming Italian paintings, all labelled as the works of Italian masters from the thirteenth to the seventeenth centuries. At last they had come to a door, over which was written in letters of German Gothic gold: 'Sala di Piero della Francesca.' The room was brilliantly lit by gas lights reflected in a giant mirror, its walls lined with yellow silk and a multi-coloured marble floor. Two sides were covered by two huge gilded, framed frescoes of men at arms, motionless, killing without expression as they stood petrified in life or death. Mr O'Neill did not try to conceal his pride and pleasure as he told how he had rescued them from a derelict church near Arezzo, ending with quiet pride: 'They complete my collection.' His enthusiasm was catching, and the little Bronson, gazing up in delight, concentrated, trying to merge his feelings with those of the artist. How ignorant he had been, his knowledge limited to indifferent art books, the whims of teachers and the inadequate museums of Boston. But as he stared, his excitement and enthusiasm abated, contradicting expectations. He felt disillusioned as he looked for what he slowly realized was not there.

His critical reverie was interrupted by his host remarking in a friendly manner: 'Well, Mr Bronson, you have certainly examined my masterpiece with care, might I ask you what conclusions you have reached?'

A voice replied before he realized it was his: 'I believe it has been repainted, little of the original painting remains.'

The art master made a gesture of irritation, the other boys frowned. Mr O'Neill stood quite still, except for his right hand tapping the pince-nez against his chest, as he pulled the thin black cord of silk tightly down. At length, he spoke: 'Thank you, sir, for your honest opinion, I am sorry you disagree with the conclusions of those accepted as experts in this neglected period of painting.' Without looking back he moved on. Bronson understood that he had offended a man he wished to please, and blushed with shame as they left the house, when the art master told him plainly he had made a discourteous fool of himself.

Later that evening as he lay on one of the lower of the double iron bunks in the small bedroom he shared with his three brothers, he regretted his rudeness. He knew he was right, but what good was that! He would never be asked again to a house in which, for the first time, he had glimpsed a way of life and a background of beauty and culture which was, he realized, his spiritual home. His reaction had been to offend the courteous, friendly owner of this paradise. His regret was unbearable, he tossed and turned but could not sleep. At last, he could bear it no longer and, getting quietly out of bed, lit a candle and in the dim light opened a little leather trunk, took out a piece of cut art paper, and wrote a letter of apology for his thoughtless rudeness and of appreciation of all the beautiful things he had seen. He licked the envelope and looked around at the walls – filthy despite all his mother's cleaning – at his brothers breathing heavily, curled up under worn, grey blankets, and compared the whole with what he had seen in the afternoon. Closing his eyes, he prayed that one day he might own such a house and fill it with perfect unrestored statues and paintings, undefiled by some coarse, uncomprehending hand.

Climbing back into his bunk, he had drawn his knees up and hugged them to his chest, trying to conceal himself in a self-made womb from the recollections of his mistakes. As he lay there, sad and despairing, he made a resolution from which he had never deviated, to make enough money to own such a palace, to abandon his plans to be a philosopher and teacher. Once he had made up his mind, he remembered, all his problems faded and he fell into a deep sleep.

But the next morning he had walked sadly to school, his confidence vanished, seeing no future except in the depressing world of business. Then he had pinched himself; he would succeed. He would make money as an art dealer. Looking back as he sat slumped at the back of the carriage, he thought how easy it had seemed to a boy. How could he have understood that the man would be haunted by an unconquerable belief that truth and beauty were inextricably intertwined, and the acceptance of double standards was self-betrayal.

These sad recollections clouded his face, giving to it an air of resigned nobility that confounded Mario who, in the church, had marvelled at the manner in which the little bearded man had taken charge of the proceedings; words spoken gently had the authority of commands. That he could want the dark and dirty lunette was incomprehensible. He could have told him of at least ten churches with finer ones, but he had wanted it; he had it and now, instead of appearing triumphant, he sat depressed.

Mario shrugged his shoulders as he looked from side to side: there was nothing interesting to see. How he hated rich English and American visitors and the way in which they went around the countryside looking at draughty, broken-down remote houses, saying how perfect they were – why didn't they live in them then? Then they spent huge sums of money on pictures of the Virgin, in whom many of them did not believe. Why buy pictures you could see for nothing in every church, why waste money which would buy vineyards and oxen? They pretended to love the sunshine, how would they like breaking earth for endless hours, while the sun burnt all the life out of you, and why, if they loved the sunshine so much, did they carry umbrellas to keep it off? No, they were mad, but he would still like to go to America and marry a beautiful fair-haired girl, who would be waiting for him every evening when he came home after making thousands of dollars. He had been confident that morning all would be well and then he had looked into Bronson's eyes! But now his confidence returned; the little man looked so sad and small, perhaps he could be pushed into doing the right thing. Was he ill, he wondered, and decided to speak before they reached home.

But Bronson had fallen again into a depressing reverie in which he watched himself washed helpless down the river of his past life. Again, he remembered the terrible poverty of his childhood, as always the visit to Mr O'Neill, his petty triumphs at Harvard, his first trip to Italy where he had lost his heart and nearly died of joy. Then followed his social successes in New York and the great country and seaside palaces of the rich where he had delighted in the luxury, the deferential servants, the respect with which he was treated. But always, at the end of every avenue, was his Eldorado, the house near Florence. From the windows of the library he would see in the centre of a cool dark circle of cypresses a marble fountain. He would watch the rising and falling water as he passed on to his disciples the knowledge and understanding which nature had given him as an extra sense. Then came the cloud of endless argument. Was he justified in achieving contentment by selling Americans Titians as Giorgiones? What could it matter, they wanted names, not works of art. Already, he had conceived a new language, or rather a use of old words expressing new meanings; conveying to those who wished to learn in simple phraseology the inspirations of art and beauty. This was the time for simplification, no longer should the select write for the select, he would explain clearly, as only those who understand can, how to look, study and approach. Explain how art was only a transfiguration of life and nature, comprehensible to all; to be enjoyed, not feared. Once this was understood, uncomprehended areas of life would be opened up to the newly educated classes and their minds elevated and broadened by the life-enhancing qualities of beauty. This new understanding must justify the means by which he could achieve it, the argument was conclusive but never did it satisfy a nagging feeling of guilt, an eternal self-distaste lingering on in his mind, poisoning his conscience, whenever he progressed towards his ambition by profitable commercial deals.

The ensuing black moods the year before, when he had other trials, had become intolerable. In desperation, he had taken advice and travelled to Vienna to talk to a professor. They had shaken hands and sat down on either side of a large desk. Bronson was immediately conscious he was being observed and evaluated in the same way as he evaluated strangers. The reversal of the normal disturbed him, he found himself resenting the calm, dispassionate examination, the enlarged elongated eyes distorted by the thick glasses into quivering fish, but he forced himself to look down and relate, with precision and accuracy, his troubles.

They talked for an hour, then the professor had said, or he remembered him to have said: 'I may be able to help you by suggesting how you can help yourself. You have been given by nature an understanding and sensibility enabling you to understand beauty. The price, or cost, of your talent is dissatisfaction with anything except perfect truth. You will never be able to divorce yourself from this characteristic or rather, I would say, quality. It is a part of your nature. You should understand, you of all men cannot live happily with self-deception.'

He had spoken slowly, and added gently: 'I would say the privations you suffered as a child, the hardships of your youth, have implanted in you an ambition to succeed. This irresistible force would suit many temperaments, but to you it appears unconsciously not as a virtue but as a continual conflict with your ideal of a fundamental purity. I believe your ambition will always defeat your idealism, but never altogether; a perpetual remnant remaining as a cancer to destroy the pleasure of your material successes. This will be the pattern of your life, destroying your peace of mind; to such an extent that even to live will at times be unbearable. So if you ask me to cure you, I cannot, you are incurable, but I would suggest you may mitigate your difficulties by cultivating an image. Try and conceive yourself by a section of coastline or seashore which you know and love. In your case,' he added with a faint smile, 'it will probably be somewhere in Europe. Picture the tide advancing slowly over sand to its highest level, conceive the water as your own self-criticism. After a time, the sea no longer advances but withdraws and with it, if you are fortunate, should retreat your blackest thoughts; but, above all, face the truth on every occasion, even if it shows you in a discreditable light.'

Bronson had taken this advice and had frequently conjured up the tides at Mont St Michel, finding perversely that the memory of the blinding speed of the incoming water relieved his feelings.

But today his thoughts would turn, despite his resistance, to the banks of the Severn. He had been taken to the riverside, almost protesting, one spring evening four years ago after a visit to Berkeley Castle, to see the incoming bore. Uninterested, he expected little, but the distant roar, the sudden rush of the great wall of water had amazed and excited him. Today the scene was repeated, but with a difference: the wall, having passed, did not roll on to disappear in the distance but remained a few yards from him seething and foaming, appearing to be pulling and sucking him in to immerse him for ever. A sense of desperation overcame him.

Suddenly into his dream, dissolving the wave like sun the mist, came the voice of Mario who, seeing the towers of Siena, had at last plucked up courage to speak (St Catherine had nodded to his mother): 'I want money to go to America, to New York, and help when I arrive there,' he said in a loud, nervous voice, his sentence fading away.

Bronson gave a little start and turned and looked at him with eyes so dispassionate that Mario felt his confidence vanishing like water out of a broken bowl. Ah what a fool he had been to listen to his mother; when he got home he'd tell her he was going to leave and marry, it didn't matter whom as long as it hurt her feelings.

Bronson continued to look quietly at Mario. Certainly he was occasionally quick-witted, but superficial, callow and uninteresting, and would never succeed either in America or in Italy. Good-looking, he would find wherever he went some woman who would look after him with false meekness, accepting the responsibility of his mistakes, and gradually take over his whole life. His shallow nature rebelling at domination, he would replace his lost confidence by getting drunk and making advances to young girls. There was nothing to like or admire in his character, nothing to hope for in his future.

'Signore,' Mario began again in a strangled voice.

'Yes,' said Bronson, raising his hand, 'I will give you a ticket and see you have the opportunity to work.' He made the promise quietly, without hope or pity, he wasn't even certain why, was it gratitude for breaking for the second time into his nightmare? Was it an attempt to change his mood? But, having spoken, he felt uncertainty vanish and self-confidence tell him that he was wise to have ambitions, to make money, to buy his villa, to write, and teach.

A weight was lifted off his shoulders as he decided to spend one more night in Siena and tomorrow hire the carriage again and, without Mario, drive to the little church of St Dorothea in the empty country north of Pienza. With him he would take one of the bright, shiny new madonnas with the gilt crowns which he kept stored for such eventualities in Siena. It would be exchanged for another dirty old picture which he was sure when cleaned would turn out to be by Sassetta. He would add it to the eight pictures he owned in the vaults of the bank in Florence. Already he knew exactly where they would hang in his villa, he gave a little smile. As to Mario, his jaw had dropped at Mr Bronson's proposal, but he quickly put on a dignified face to hide his desire to laugh, dance and sing. Twice he had to turn his back on his companion to lean over the side and pretend to examine the wheels to hide the smile of sheer delight that kept breaking through his mask. Now he would leave Italy, soon he would be a millionaire, with a special train and a beautiful wife and a huge house in which his mother would have rooms of her own upstairs. In twenty years' time they would all come back to Siena and have a happy old age, looked up to and respected by those who now treated them with disdain.

As the carriage slowly climbed the hill the two men, differing in their thoughts, hopes and ambitions, sat contented with each other and as happy as their self-deceptions and delusions were ever to allow them to be.